W9-BFG-294

"You make me break every promise to myself.

I promise myself that I won't like you," Daisy continued. "I tell myself that one night with you is enough, that it's all I need. And then…and then you ruin it all. Worse than that, you make me indecisive. I'm not indecisive, Jacob, I don't make an important decision and then change my mind because of a kiss."

"Are you inviting me in?" Jacob rested his forehead against hers.

"I am."

"If I come inside, I won't leave until morning."

"You better not," she said. "And I do hope you're more prepared than you were last time."

"I'm ever the optimist, so yes."

Daisy pulled Jacob inside by the tie. "You and your suits," she said as she closed and locked the door behind him. "Take it off."

Dear Reader,

Small-town living in the South is rife with possibilities when it comes to writing romance. There are characters everywhere you turn, families who have made their mark, men and women who have chosen to make themselves a part of a community where everyone knows everyone else and secrets are hard to keep. A beauty shop and small-engine-repair business is not at all a stretch, when it comes to small towns everywhere.

Family is important to me, as it is to Daisy Bell and Jacob Tasker in this story. They're both willing to make sacrifices for family members, to endure personal pain in order to make life easier for those they love. But after making those sacrifices for others, is it time to let the mistakes of the past go and take time for themselves? Can they find a second chance at love?

I hope you enjoy your journey into Bell Grove, Georgia, and the chance to watch Daisy and Jacob find one another all over again.

Happy reading!

Linda

A WEEK TILL
THE WEDDING

LINDA WINSTEAD JONES

HARLEQUIN®

entertain, enrich, inspire™

If you purchased this book without a cover you should be aware
that this book is stolen property. It was reported as "unsold and
destroyed" to the publisher, and neither the author nor the
publisher has received any payment for this "stripped book."

Recycling programs
for this product may
not exist in your area.

ISBN-13: 978-0-373-65689-9

A WEEK TILL THE WEDDING

Copyright © 2012 by Linda Winstead Jones

All rights reserved. Except for use in any review, the reproduction
or utilization of this work in whole or in part in any form by any
electronic, mechanical or other means, now known or hereafter
invented, including xerography, photocopying and recording, or in
any information storage or retrieval system, is forbidden without
the written permission of the publisher, Harlequin Enterprises Limited,
225 Duncan Mill Road, Don Mills, Ontario M3B 3K9, Canada.

This is a work of fiction. Names, characters, places and incidents are
either the product of the author's imagination or are used fictitiously, and
any resemblance to actual persons, living or dead, business establishments,
events or locales is entirely coincidental.

This edition published by arrangement with Harlequin Books S.A.

For questions and comments about the quality of this book please contact us
at Customer_eCare@Harlequin.ca.

® and TM are trademarks of Harlequin Enterprises Limited or its corporate
affiliates. Trademarks indicated with ® are registered in the United States Patent
and Trademark Office, the Canadian Trade Marks Office and in other countries.

www.Harlequin.com

Printed in U.S.A.

LINDA WINSTEAD JONES

is a bestselling author of more than fifty romance books in several subgenres—historical, fairy tale, paranormal and, of course, romance suspense. She's won a Colorado Romance Writers Award of Excellence twice. She is also a three-time RITA® Award finalist and (writing as Linda Fallon) winner of the 2004 RITA® Award for paranormal romance.

Linda lives in north Alabama with her husband of thirty-seven years. She can be reached via www.Harlequin.com or her own website, www.lindawinsteadjones.com.

For my niece Christy, a hairstylist who keeps me from going gray and living in ponytails. She hasn't yet added small-engine repair, but…maybe someday. :-) Love you!

Chapter One

"Those women on Crime Stoppers never have good haircuts. Have you noticed? Maybe if they didn't look so unkempt they'd make better choices. You know, get a job, marry a decent man. Just look at those bangs, bless her heart." Sandra Miller was a talker; Daisy never had to work to make conversation when Sandra was in the chair getting her hair done.

Daisy paused, scissors in hand, and glanced over the top of her client's head to catch a glimpse of a mug shot on the twenty-inch television that was mounted on the wall. Bell Grove, Georgia, was a small town off the beaten path, north of Atlanta. They didn't have their own television station, but they picked up the Atlanta stations. "Yeah, those bangs are pretty bad."

"A woman just can't feel good about herself if her hair looks that awful." Sandra gestured to the television. "I swear, I'd be tempted to use drugs myself if I had bangs like that. She has to have something to dull the pain."

Another mug shot was flashed on the screen. "Oh, dear," Sandra said softly. "Her problems go so far beyond bangs I don't know where to start. Don't they sell conditioner in Atlanta? And what color *is* that, exactly? I have never seen a box of Miss Clairol with *orange* or *pumpkin* stamped on it." In the mirror, Sandra caught and held Daisy's eye. "You know, you could do a lot of good, if you were of a mind to help those poor, unfortunate women. You can't overestimate how important hairstyle is to a woman's confidence."

Daisy laughed. "Sorry, Sandra. My hands are full enough without adding in the occasional trip to the Atlanta jail to give beauty advice."

Yes, her hands were more than full enough. Daisy was the sole proprietor of Bell's Beauty Shop and Small Engine Repair. She had no employees, though her sister Mari— the youngest of the three Bell girls—came home on the weekends to help with the repair aspect of the business. Mari was in junior college, and Lily had recently started a new job in an Atlanta art gallery. Lily didn't make it to Bell Grove as often as she had when she'd been a student. These days her weekends were taken up with the new job and new friends and settling into her new apartment.

While Daisy missed seeing her sisters on a regular basis, it wasn't like she didn't have enough to do. In addition to the business, which kept her busy enough since it was Bell Grove's only beauty salon and repair shop, she did volunteer work. On Mondays, when her shop was closed, she delivered meals to a number of housebound residents in the county. Some were elderly, others were in bad health; a couple had just fallen on hard times and needed a little help. While she wasn't keen on the idea of inspiring prisoners to change their ways by providing free haircuts, she had spent more hours than she could count spiffing up the hairstyles of those who didn't get out much. The service—the meals, not the hair trimming and restyling—was sponsored by the Bell Grove Methodist Church, as was a food bank which Daisy also volunteered for when she could.

She gave some of these same people rides to town, when she wasn't working and they needed to go to the doctor—there was a grand total of one in Bell Grove—or the grocery store. There was just the one grocery store, too. Bell Grove provided all the necessary services; there just wasn't much to choose from. Anyone who wasn't happy with their limited selection could—and did—drive into Atlanta or one of the communities between Bell Grove and the big city.

Daisy didn't get out of Bell Grove often. Everything she needed was close at hand. She liked it here, and everything she needed was within reach. Well, *almost* everything.

Sandra asked about Lily and Marigold, and Daisy filled her in on all the latest news. As she did, her heart sank a little. Just a little. She tried not to let her sad reaction show. When their parents had been killed Daisy had stepped up and done what needed to be done. She'd put her life on hold, sacrificing her own plans to take care of her younger sisters. Lily and Mari had still been in school at the time, Lily in the county high school, Mari in the middle school. There had been no close relatives to take over as guardian to the younger girls, so that duty had fallen to Daisy. Now they were grown, they had lives of their own.

That was as it should be, right? But sometimes Daisy felt as if she was suffering from Empty Nest Syndrome at the ripe old age of twenty-eight.

She never would've considered staying in Bell Grove and taking over her parents' businesses if they'd lived.

Her plans had been grander than that. A college degree—she'd waffled between physical therapy and elementary education and had finally decided on education—and a job in the big city. Marriage, babies, the PTA and Little League. Maybe her plans had not been grand, but they'd been *hers*. More than once in the past seven years she'd spent a sleepless night wondering where she'd be if that eighteen-wheeler hadn't crossed the center line. She would've finished college, gotten that job, made a life of her own. Would she have been as content with that life as she was with this one? Would things have turned out as she'd planned? She'd stopped asking those questions years ago. There was no way to know what that alternate life might've been like; there was no upside for her in "what-if?"

She liked her life just fine, and those old plans seemed so distant they might as well have been someone else's.

Daisy gave Sandra's new, shorter cut a good blow-dry with a round brush, touched it up with a spritz of hair spray and whipped off the purple cape that had protected her client's clothing. Sandra was happy with the new style, and had just begun to gush about how much slimmer her face looked with the new cut when the door to the shop opened. Daisy didn't have anyone scheduled for another hour. She'd planned to grab a sandwich as soon as Sandra left. But she did take walk-ins, and since business wasn't exactly booming she'd gladly skip lunch to squeeze in another haircut. Maybe someone was dropping off a small item for repair, though if that was the case...

That was as far as her thoughts wandered before the person who'd opened the door stepped inside.

Jacob Tasker, the biggest "what-if?" of them all, looked her in the eye the way he always had, with confidence in his steady gaze. Dark brown eyes, like strong black coffee, caught hers and held on. He was bigger than he'd been when she'd last seen him. Not in a bad way; he didn't have the beginnings of a gut, or jowls, or a double chin. All through college he'd bordered on skinny. He'd been wiry, at the very least. Since then he'd put on a few pounds of muscle, filling his expensive suit well.

Not only did that suit cost more than she made in a month, but no one wore a suit in Bell Grove unless A) They were Mayor or B) It was Sunday.

His haircut was expensive, too. There wasn't a single hair out of place, no misbehaving cowlick or split ends. He was recently well-shaven. Damned if he couldn't've just stepped out of an ad for expensive cologne or a ridiculously overpriced watch. And that smile…even though she could tell it was somewhat forced, the smile hadn't changed at all. That smile had captured her when she'd been fifteen and he'd been eighteen. She'd fallen hard. She'd doodled *Mrs. Daisy Tasker* on the inside cover, and numerous pages, of every notebook and journal she'd owned, with swirly hearts over the *i* in Daisy. At that time he'd been too old for her, and she'd never confessed her feelings to anyone, not even to her closest friends. He'd been her secret crush, her heart's deepest desire.

Four years later, when she'd been nineteen and he'd been twenty-two, they'd attended the same college and the three-year age difference was no longer an impediment. Since he'd taken a year off between high school and college, and he'd changed his major—twice—they'd even had some classes together. The smile had done her in again, along with other attributes she hadn't been able to even imagine at fifteen. That had been a blissfully happy time of her life; she'd lived in a fairy tale.

And a little less than two years later it had all fallen

apart, and she'd been reminded that the original fairy tales always had a wicked twist at the end.

Crap. Daisy couldn't say she hadn't ever imagined seeing Jacob again, but in her fantasy she'd had time to put on something pretty and freshen her makeup. She'd been ridiculously happy; she hadn't missed him *at all*. In her daydreams she could barely remember what he looked like. She had no regrets, there were no "what-ifs?" On the other hand he'd been miserable, so very sorry he'd let her slip away. In her imaginings he had not aged well. Maybe there was a gut, or a softening of his features. Just enough of an unflattering change to make her glad that their relationship had ended when it had. Ah, fantasy.

But in real life she was wearing a minimum of makeup and a black smock over well-worn jeans and a sadly old Brooks and Dunn T-shirt. And he looked better than she remembered, more a man, harder. Sharper. She thought about Jacob too damn often. And he didn't look at all sorry. No, he looked as confident as always, as if he never had a single moment of doubt about any decision he'd ever made.

Not even leaving her.

He closed the door on the bright sunshine, said hello to her and to Sandra, who—thankfully—prattled about how long it had been since she'd seen Jacob, how she'd heard about his success, and how was California, anyway? She asked about his brothers and his cousins. He had plenty of relatives in the area, so that took a while. While the Bells had dwindled—only the three sisters remained of the founders of this small town—the Taskers had multiplied and flourished. You couldn't take two steps in the county without tripping over one of Jacob's cousins.

While Jacob and Sandra exchanged pleasantries, Daisy took a deep breath and tried to decide what she should say, when the time for her to speak arrived. Her hands fell to her thighs, where she wiped them on her jeans. Her nails weren't painted. She had sweaty palms. Great. He couldn't have called first? He couldn't have given her a little warning so she could brush up on her speech? How rude!

As Jacob and Sandra talked, the television news droned on, the announcer's words making no sense at all. Blah, blah, blah. Yada yada yada. The air conditioner whirred. Daisy was aware of every sound that filled the room, most specifically Jacob's voice. She'd always loved his voice; the timbre, the way she felt it in her spine.

She really should pretend that seeing him again didn't affect her at all, but it was probably too late for that. Her jaw had dropped when he'd walked in and she'd stared at him wordlessly for too long to pull off that lie. He'd probably noticed her wiping her sweaty palms on her jeans; he never had been one to miss much. She could just light into him and say all the things she sometimes wished she'd said. For a long while all the things she wished she'd said to him had kept her up at night. None of them were pleasant.

But when Sandra put cash on the front counter, waved at Daisy and left, and Daisy and Jacob were left alone, what she said was,

"What the hell do you want?"

Well, what had he expected? A parade?

Daisy hadn't changed much at all. She still had long pale hair, cornflower-blue eyes, long legs and flawless, lightly tanned skin. On the drive over Jacob had wondered if Daisy would look older, if sacrificing for her family and giving up her own dreams, seven years ago, had drained her.

But she looked as good as ever. Better, in fact. The years had been good to her. The girl he'd loved was gone, replaced by a gorgeous woman.

"I need a favor," he said, suspecting that her response to that simple request wouldn't be pretty.

"A favor." She shook her head in wonder, and her posture changed as if she were getting ready to do battle. Maybe she was. "From me? Is this a joke?"

"Just hear me out."

Daisy threw up her hands. Her cheeks flushed pink. "Whatever this favor is, I don't have the time."

Bell's Beauty Shop and Small Engine Repair was located in the heart of downtown Bell Grove, on the square across from city hall, sandwiched between an antiques shop and a family-run sandwich shop. All the buildings in the downtown area were old as dirt. The owners did their best to keep them in good repair, but there was no way to disguise the effects of a hundred years plus of use.

Bell's was small but clean, the walls freshly painted a welcoming pale green, the magazines neatly stacked. The chairs in the shop were mismatched, probably yard sale finds, but somehow Daisy had made it all look planned. The lace curtains and live plants pulled it all together. There was a counter in the back, just past the door to the restroom, and a dark green wooden door that he knew opened onto the area where her dad had once fixed mowers and other lawn-care equipment, as well as the occasional toaster even though there were no small engines in kitchen appliances. Business didn't exactly seem to be brisk.

"The favor is not for me," he explained.

"Oh, really." Her voice was cool, as if she didn't care.

"It's Grandma Eunice."

Her face fell, a little. She'd always liked his dad's mother, and Grandma Eunice had liked Daisy. Which was probably a contributing factor in this latest problem.

Like it or not, he was going to have to explain. "I came home for the big family reunion, and since I haven't been back in a while I decided to stay for a month." He didn't tell her that the only reason he was here now was that his mother had told him it might be the last reunion his grandmother would see.

"Can that big company you work for survive without you for that long?" she snapped.

He'd been getting up early and staying up late to take care of business via cell phone and computer while he was here, but that detail wasn't relevant. Might as well just get to the heart of the matter. "Grandma Eunice isn't well."

Daisy's face paled a little. She couldn't have known. The Taskers and the Bells weren't exactly the Hatfields and the McCoys, but they didn't run in the same circles, either.

"I'm sorry to hear Miss Eunice is not well," Daisy said, her voice cool but not without genuine sympathy.

"Physically she doesn't seem to be in bad shape, though she's not getting around the way she used to. She's been in a wheelchair for a while. But her mind…" Might as well spit it out. "Daisy, she thinks we're engaged and she's been asking about you."

Daisy had never had much of a poker face. Her blue eyes widened, her mouth puckered slightly. Maybe she even paled, a bit. Her pretty mouth opened and closed a couple of times before she asked, "Is it Alzheimer's?"

"The doctor says no."

"Then what…"

"She doesn't forget everything, she's functions very well and remembers what she had for breakfast, but there are certain times when her memory just seems to malfunction. She has a terrible time remembering Ben's wife, but most specifically, her memory malfunctions where I'm concerned."

Daisy looked as confused as he'd been feeling for the

past few days. "You'll just have to tell her the truth," she said.

If only it were that simple. "I did. I told her we broke up a long time ago, that we were never engaged. She got upset, I went to the kitchen to make her some hot tea, and when I got back she was completely calm. Smiling, serene, looking out her bedroom window. I thought she was fine, that she'd accepted the truth, but…" The matter still concerned him. "She'd forgotten. In just a few minutes' time, she completely forgot what I'd told her about us." He bit the bullet and dropped the bombshell. "She's planning our wedding."

Daisy reached out to steady herself by grabbing the edge of the counter. Jacob considered stepping forward to take her arm, but he quickly thought better of it.

"What do you expect me to do?" she asked, her voice rising sharply. "I can't…we can't…this is not my problem!"

"I don't expect you to marry me to keep my grandmother happy," Jacob said sharply. "But if you would play along for a while, come to the family reunion if she keeps this up, maybe hang out at the house when you can. She might wake up one morning and have forgotten all about this fantasy of hers, but at the very least once I'm gone she'll let it go." Out of sight, out of mind. "She's promised to see a new doctor, but not until *after* the reunion."

"Play. Along." Ah, there was the difference in Daisy, *that's* how she'd changed. Her eyes were harder, more cynical. They'd never looked at him like this before.

"It would make an old woman very happy. She adores you."

"Give me a break. You aren't doing this for *her*. No, you want me to get *you* off the hook so you won't have to try again to tell her that we're not getting married. Heaven forbid that Jacob Tasker should have to do anything that he finds unpleasant. Heaven forbid that anything that's not in your precious plans…" She stopped, choking on her words.

Jacob took a deep breath, he exhaled slowly. He wished—not for the first time—that he was back in San Francisco, where his days and the decisions he had to make made sense. This situation was maddening. "I've been home four days, and I've told Grandma Eunice ten times that we're not engaged and never were. She's upset by the news, and then a few minutes later she forgets. I'm getting damn tired of upsetting her again and again."

Daisy was already shaking her head.

"I'll pay you."

There were those daggers in her eyes again. Her posture changed, as if she were literally getting ready to attack. "You think you can buy me off? That I'll do anything for money? Oh, poor Daisy Bell, she'll do anything for a few bucks."

He'd be glad to pay her more than a "few bucks." And it looked as if she could use the money. Jacob had put Daisy firmly in his rearview mirror years ago, but he hated the idea that she didn't have more. She'd sacrificed a lot for her sisters; she'd given up her own education, the career she'd planned. She'd raised Lily and Mari, put them through college, and from all he could see she'd done nothing for herself. Why in hell was she still here? She should've moved on years ago.

He snapped out a ridiculously high amount, a number large enough to make Daisy take a stutter-step back.

"Are you insane?" she asked.

No, he wasn't insane; he was ridiculously rich. He worked eighty to ninety hours a week, and until now he hadn't taken a real vacation since he'd gone to work for The Hudson-Dahlgren Corporation seven years ago. He'd become a workaholic who had no time for anything else. But all his hard work had paid off. Very well.

"I'm afraid Grandma Eunice doesn't have much time left. She's deteriorated so much since I last saw her. Physically, mentally...the doctor says it's manageable, but I don't buy it." He'd talked to her doctor—an old codger who wasn't much younger than she was—and according to the doc there was nothing to be done. Eunice Tasker was simply growing old. Jacob had initially offered to bring in specialists, to fly his grandmother to a decent hospital for tests and treatment, but she'd refused both offers. *After* the reunion, she'd said, she'd see a new doctor. Maybe her mind was slipping, but she was as stubborn as ever.

"You could help to make her final days happy ones." And he could leave here knowing Daisy was in good financial shape. She could finish school, close this crappy shop, get out of town the way he had.

She considered his offer for a long moment, and finally said, "All right, I'll help. A couple of visits to your grandmother, a few lies...I can do that." She walked toward him, came close, reached out and punched him in the chest with the tip of her index finger. She didn't look him in the eye as she poked him there, hard.

Jacob didn't move, but he took a long, deep breath. Damn, she smelled good. The sight of Daisy brought back strong, old memories, but it was the way she smelled that triggered memories he had no right to cling to. She was the stuff of dreams, the kind of woman a man could never entirely let go of, no matter how hard he tried.

"But I won't take a dime of your money," she said. "I'm doing this for Miss Eunice, not for you. She was kind to me after my parents died. She's a good woman and I'll do this for *her*." Daisy lifted her head slowly, until her eyes met his. "Not for you and not for your money." She said the word "money" as if it was a bad thing.

He'd change her mind about the money, eventually, but he wasn't going to argue with her now.

"Dinner tonight with the family?"

"Not wasting any time, are you?" she countered.

"Might as well not."

After seeing her, smelling her, remembering their time together—the good and the bad—he knew the sooner they got this over with, the better off they'd both be.

Their time, their chance, had come and gone years ago. He didn't pine for anything or anyone, but a small, reluctant part of his brain recognized that Daisy Bell disturbed him on some primitive level. He didn't need or want to be dragged into the past, not by old memories, not by a surprisingly tantalizing scent.

Daisy was the past, and Jacob cared only about the present and the future. Only a fool would be tempted by something long gone.

Chapter Two

The Taskers had been movers and shakers in the county for as long as there'd been a county. The family home, a few miles out of Bell Grove, was stately and majestic and yet still homey. It wasn't a showplace, it was a home. At least, it had been home years ago when Daisy had come here often with Jacob as his girlfriend. Holidays, summer vacations…for nearly two years she'd spent much of her time away from school and her part-time job with her parents right here. She'd never told anyone how much she loved this old house. And she never would.

Through the years residents had tried to give it an appropriate name, a name befitting a fine home with a rich history. Now and then a Tasker would try to call it Magnolia Whatsit or Oak Something. But what it was always called, what stuck, was Tasker House. Daisy had always thought that made the fabulous, sprawling two-story mansion sound like something out of an Edgar Allen Poe story.

Apparently she was not alone in that belief, and that was why Taskers kept trying to change it.

For the occasion, Daisy had chosen her outfit carefully. She wanted to look good, for the family and even for Jacob, though where he was concerned it was intended in a "this is what you threw away, look but don't touch" kind of way. She wore a pale green sundress that hit the top of her knees, white sandals, and her hair down. Maybe she hadn't done anything spectacular with her hair, but she'd brushed until it gleamed. Jacob had looked at her more often than was necessary on the ride from town, cutting his eyes from the road now and then to study her. It was what she'd wanted, right? She wanted him to regret giving her up, she wanted him to suffer.

So why was she determined to meet him here next time and avoid being trapped in a car with him again?

The way he stared at her made her squirm. Sitting so close to him for so long was making her seriously antsy. In trying to punish him, she had ended up punishing herself. It was absolute torture to have him so close. And he didn't seem to be tortured *at all*.

The house was just as she remembered it, majestic and welcoming, perfectly positioned on a vast expanse of land that was lushly green. A portion of the land was flat and had once been farmed, but to the west there were gentle hills and ancient trees. She and Jacob had taken many a long walk in those hills…

He offered his arm at the porch steps, and she took it. She would not allow him to see how she was affected by his closeness. He couldn't know, not ever, that he made her squirm.

"Do you sleep in a suit?" she asked coolly as they walked up the steps, neither of them in a hurry. He looked good in the dark suit and crisp white shirt, she'd admit, especially since everything he had on fit him as if it had been made for his body, but the outfit seemed wrong here at Tasker House, especially given the season. Even late in the day, the summer heat remained. And the humidity... you could not dismiss the humidity! Besides, the stupid suit reminded her that he'd dumped her for his precious career. She didn't want or need his success rubbed in her face.

"Not usually," he said.

She shouldn't have asked that question. As she recalled, he usually slept in nothing at all. At least, he had when she'd been around. So had she, come to think of it. They hadn't lived together, though that step had been coming, but she'd spent the night at his place and he'd spent the night at hers—when roommates were away. It was a vivid memory she could do without, given the circumstances. She tried to think of other things, to push the memory of a naked Jacob out of her mind, but nothing else would stick.

Before she could wipe the image of a naked Jacob from her brain, Susan Tasker met them at the door. The screen door squealed as she opened it, and she smiled. Or tried. It was the most pathetic attempt at a smile Daisy had ever seen. Focusing on Jacob's mother helped; it was difficult to fantasize about the man naked while the woman Daisy had once believed would one day be her mother-in-law looked on.

Susan Tasker had married into the prominent and wealthy Tasker family, but she'd soon become one of its leaders. Her husband, Jim, Miss Eunice's only living child, was a quiet man who seemed to be happy to share the handling of the family business matters and properties with his wife. She had given him four sons and taken on an active role in the multiple Tasker concerns—there were a number of businesses across the South that were at least partially owned by the family corporation—as if she'd been born to it.

And now she cared for his mother, as well.

"Daisy," she said softly as she backed up to allow her and Jacob to enter the house.

"Mrs. Tasker."

The older woman—she had to be approaching sixty—turned around, waving a hand dismissively. "Oh, call me Susan. You're not a child any longer."

Susan had put on a few pounds in the years since Daisy had seen her, and whoever was styling her hair had done a terrible job. The color was flat and lifeless, and the cut was too severe for the shape of her face. She needed layering, and some highlights to soften the color.

Which was, Daisy reminded herself as they followed Susan Tasker toward the parlor, *not* her problem.

From first glance, it was clear to her that the house hadn't changed. Not a stick of furniture from the entryway had been moved, and she would swear that even the fresh flowers on the round table near the foot of the staircase were exactly the same as they'd been last time she was here. The ceilings were high, the furnishings antique, the pictures unexciting landscapes and old family portraits framed in gold. This place was a constant, never changing.

She loved this old house, even though Taskers lived in it.

Jim Tasker was in the parlor, enjoying a predinner drink. Jacob's youngest brother Ben was there with his wife, Madison. And Eunice Tasker sat in the center of the room. She managed to look stately and dignified, even though she was seated in a wheelchair. Even though she did not look well.

It broke Daisy's heart a little to see the elderly woman so confined, and so obviously unwell. Her color was sallow, her hands unsteady. Her face was more deeply lined than it had been the last time Daisy had seen her. Like Susan, she could use a decent haircut.

Eunice's face lit up when she saw Daisy and Jacob. She smiled, the expression erasing years from her wrinkled face. A little color crept into her cheeks. "Oh, I'm so glad you're finally here," she said, her eyes on Daisy. "We have so much to discuss!"

Daisy walked to Eunice, bent and kissed her on the cheek. The old woman smelled like baby powder and flowery perfume, and her skin was papery soft. Standing there, the last of her doubts about this ridiculous scheme fled. She'd do this, no matter how painful it might be. And she was *not* doing it for Jacob. "Miss Eunice, it's been too long."

"Yes, it's been several weeks, hasn't it?" Eunice said, taking Daisy's hands in her own. "That is far too long."

Daisy just smiled. It had been years, not weeks, but she wouldn't distress the ill woman with inconvenient facts.

Miss Eunice squeezed Daisy's hand. "You look even more beautiful than I remember." Her gaze—those eyes dark, like Jacob's—flitted past Daisy to look upon her grandson. "Doesn't your lovely bride-to-be get more beautiful every day?"

"Yes, she does," Jacob agreed solemnly.

"She's going to be stunning in my wedding gown."

The entire room went silent. Of course, everyone there but Eunice knew Daisy's relationship with Jacob had been over for a very long time. How hard must this be for the family?

Daisy couldn't feel too bad for them. This ruse was harder on her than it could possibly be on anyone else. She had to pretend not to hate Jacob for moving on without her, for not giving up his dreams for her the way she had given up hers for her sisters. He'd chosen his precious career over her. His determination to succeed at anything he chose to do had been one of the things she'd always admired about him, but in the end that determination had taken him away from her.

And then she looked around the room, taking in the pale faces, the thinned lips, the clasped hands. The Taskers were losing a beloved member of their family, not quickly and without warning, the way she'd lost her parents, but slowly. Painfully. And she had the power to make Miss Eunice's final days happier. Not for them, she reminded herself, but for a woman who had been good to the Bell family for as long as Daisy could remember.

She smiled, looking at Miss Eunice and ignoring the others. "I can't wait to see the gown. I'm sure it's lovely."

"Tonight, after dinner," Miss Eunice said with barely contained glee. "You must try the gown on! We have to make sure it fits properly."

It was as if the old woman was trying to make this as difficult as possible. Everything was happening too fast as it was! "Oh, there's no rush," Daisy said, making a real effort to keep her voice calm. The idea of trying on a family wedding gown, when at one time she had been so sure that one day this would be *her* family, was enough to give her hives.

Eunice leaned forward, gripping the armrests of her wheelchair. "No rush? What if alterations are necessary? And don't forget, we must choose a new veil that will complement the gown and your face. So much to do, so very much to do. If the wedding is going to take place during the Tasker Reunion in less than three weeks, we haven't a single day to waste."

"What?" She and Jacob responded in stereo.

"Surprise!" Eunice said brightly.

* * *

Jacob held his spine straight and kept his face impassive. In a few hours Grandma Eunice would forget that Daisy had been here. She'd definitely forget about a wedding she'd planned to be held during the reunion. In two and a half weeks. The delusion had come to life when she'd seen him, and it would go away just as suddenly, when something else grabbed her attention.

Daisy looked like she'd seen a ghost, and in a way she had. For a couple of years she'd been a part of this family. For close to two years he and Daisy had been together. For almost a year of that time, they'd been damn near inseparable. Christmas and Thanksgiving, family reunions, weekends at home…she'd been here. They hadn't discussed marriage, they had both been too young. But she'd fit in so well here, she'd become like a member of the family. Everyone had loved her. Including him.

Maybe they hadn't discussed marriage, but he couldn't say it hadn't been a part of his plans. He was certain it had been a part of her plans, too.

And then her parents had been killed and everything had changed.

Jacob had tried to be there for Daisy. He'd held her while she'd cried; he'd stayed with her through the funeral arrangements and—later—the legal details of the estate and guardianship. But eventually his new job had called him away, and he'd gone. He'd truly believed that they would be able to make a long distance relationship work until the time came when Daisy—and her sisters—joined him. The job offer he'd received had been too good to turn down, it had been exciting and he'd made enough money right off the bat to support himself, Daisy and her sisters. All he had to do was get settled and send for her.

But it hadn't worked that way. There hadn't been any

spectacular blowup, no emotional scene. They'd simply drifted apart. It had been easy to do, with him working night and day in San Francisco and Daisy caught up in raising her sisters and taking over the family businesses here in Bell Grove, Georgia. Her dad had trained the girls from the time they could walk to tune an engine. Beauty school had taken care of the rest. If she'd come to San Francisco or if he'd stayed here, maybe they'd still be together. But she hadn't and he hadn't. And they weren't.

So here they were, seven years later. They'd both changed. Everything had changed. Well, perhaps not *everything*. Jacob was annoyed to admit that he wanted Daisy. She wasn't like any other woman. She could look at him, and he felt it to the bone.

A long time ago he'd convinced himself he was over her, but as soon as he'd laid eyes on her he'd realized how wrong he'd been. If he was over her, the curve of her cheek and the sway of her hips when she walked wouldn't drive him wild. If he was over her, he wouldn't continually find himself edging closer so he could inhale her scent. Dammit, he wasn't *over her* at all.

The past was coming back to bite him in the ass, even though logically he knew they were no longer the same people. If he spent a significant amount of time with Daisy he'd soon realize that they had grown apart. He wasn't the same; neither was she. Whatever he felt was annoyingly lingering chemistry. Nothing more.

It was announced that dinner was on the table, thank goodness, ending the conversation about wedding gowns and family reunions and surprise ceremonies. Jacob took Daisy's arm and escorted her to the dining room, hoping that the meal would serve as a distraction. He didn't miss the slight tremble of her body, even though outwardly she did her best to remain calm. Dammit, he shouldn't have asked her to do this. He should've found a way to take care of the situation without asking Daisy to torture herself.

And him.

His mom didn't cook, but that didn't mean the family didn't eat well. Lurlene Preston had been in charge of the kitchen for thirty years, and no one cooked a good old-fashioned Southern meal like Lurlene. The meal that was laid out was definitely a welcome distraction. Jacob didn't eat this way when he was in California. Not that he could've gotten fried chicken, turnip greens, fried okra and fried green tomatoes, served up with a mess of cornbread, in San Francisco. Even if he could've found those foods in a specialty restaurant, they wouldn't have been the same. The smells and tastes transported him back to his childhood, to family dinners followed by the front porch swing or an hour or so spent working on whatever car he was remodeling at the time.

He and Caleb—they were the middle boys of the four, and Caleb was almost two years older than Jacob—had both had an interest in rebuilding cars from the age of fourteen or so on. It was something they'd enjoyed doing together, even though they didn't have much else in common. Jacob hadn't touched an engine since he'd moved to San Francisco. He didn't even change the oil in his own car. No, he paid someone else to do it for him. Jacob hadn't missed tinkering with engines at all, hadn't even thought about that old hobby until he'd come home.

Funny how the scents of his youth were the ones plaguing him this week. Food. Engine oil. Daisy. Daisy, most of all.

For a while they enjoyed a reprieve from wedding talk. Everyone talked about the weather, the food, baseball and the upcoming football season and the relatives who were not in attendance. Daisy was quiet in the beginning, and she just picked at her food. But after a while she relaxed. She ate, participated in the conversation and completely and totally ignored him.

Which was good, in one way. He could stare at her all he wanted, and she wouldn't realize that he studied the gentle curve of her jaw and the tempting length of her neck. He didn't dare look any lower—not for more than a split second here and there—for fear that she'd turn in his direction and catch him with his eyes on the swell of her breasts. He knew better. He didn't ogle women. But this was Daisy, and he might never get another chance.

Their reprieve ended as peach cobbler was served. Grandma Eunice began again to discuss her plans for the wedding. The ceremony would be held Sunday afternoon of the three-day Tasker Reunion, she'd decided. It would be the culmination of the annual event, a formal wedding to be held in the house. Family only, since space would be an issue. Besides, Grandma Eunice added with her nose in the air, family was all that mattered.

She looked at him as she added this last dig. It wasn't a secret that she was annoyed at Jacob for throwing himself so wholeheartedly into his career, for not coming home and taking his place here. The Taskers owned interests in several successful restaurants, a department store—there were three locations, now—a steel mill and a sock factory. Jacob's grandfather and great-uncles—three of them—had gone into business together. They'd done well. These days this branch of the family was the most prosperous, but Jacob had many cousins—close and distant—who continued to hold a portion of old family businesses.

He could've taken a job at any one of them, or else begun working with his mother with the objective of eventually taking the reins from her. But he was determined to make it on his own, to be independently successful. Yes, his ambition had taken him away from his family for too long, he could admit to that. Was that why when his grandmother's mind had started to go she'd immediately honed in on this wedding business? Was she, somehow, determined to see him married to a local girl before she died so he'd be tied to Bell Grove in yet another way?

Jacob had hoped his grandmother would forget about having Daisy try on her wedding dress before the meal was done, but no such luck. No, she was anxious to see Daisy in the gown, prepared to get Lurlene to take care of any alterations that might be necessary. Daisy paled at the thought, he caught a hint of a return of that tremble that told him how hard this was for her, but she played along. The four women left the table and headed for Grandma Eunice's suite of rooms. Years ago, when she'd first started having trouble with the stairs, they'd converted the library and sitting room on the ground floor for her.

When the women had gone, Jacob stared at his dad and his brother—one and then the other. "Why didn't you tell me she was this bad?" he asked, keeping his voice low.

His father shrugged his shoulders. "It happened so fast. She's had trouble remembering some things for years, but we thought it was normal, related to her aging. Then all of a sudden she's losing whole blocks of time. Months, years. The doctor says the memory loss could be caused by any number of things, but…I don't know."

Ben nodded his head. "I know we don't get here often enough, but I swear, one time when we saw her she was fine. Sharp as a tack. A couple of months later she doesn't remember who Maddy is."

They hadn't been paying attention, if they thought this had come on suddenly. That wasn't the way dementia worked, unless it was a sudden side effect of a medication or an infection. Those possibilities had been checked and rejected. Jacob couldn't very well complain to his father and younger brother about their lack of attention to the family matriarch. He hadn't been home in years, so he could hardly jump all over them for not understanding the small changes that had turned into big ones. But dammit, they were *here*.

"She needs a more competent doctor."

"Good luck getting her to agree to that," Jim grumbled.

"You have to make it happen," Jacob snapped.

"She's agreed to see someone after the reunion. She wouldn't even agree to that much until you came home. That's a step in the right direction."

A step that should've been taken months ago. Jacob decided not to argue any longer with his father, who was maddeningly laid-back about the entire situation. Arguing was a waste of breath, apparently.

"Daisy looks great!" Ben said brightly, happy to change the subject.

"Yes, she does," Jacob agreed sourly. *Too* great.

"How on earth did you get her to agree to this? I figured she'd tell you to take a hike."

He'd love to be able to tell Ben that he'd bought Daisy's cooperation, but she'd taken that option away from him. "She's doing it for Grandma Eunice, not for me. They always did get along well."

Ben snorted. "I wish she and Maddy could find a way to get along. Grandma Eunice never approved of my wife, she never liked her the way she liked Daisy. Not once did she offer to let Maddy wear her wedding dress." He shook his head. "Not that Maddy would've worn the old thing."

Ben's wife was very pretty, but she was also very flashy. Madison had made the mistake of wearing a very short dress to the house the first time she'd had dinner here.

According to Susan, Grandma Eunice had never forgiven that infraction.

The men retired to the parlor for scotch and cigars, an old tradition that had survived many, many years in this household. Jacob passed on the offered cigar but took the scotch. Just one. He had a feeling he was going to need the fortification in order to get through the rest of the evening.

Eunice watched as Daisy followed her instructions and very carefully removed the wedding gown from the wardrobe. Eunice had had the dress—more than sixty years old and as beautiful as it had been the day she'd worn it—removed from storage as soon as she'd heard that Jacob was coming home.

Daisy was a beautiful girl. More than that she was a sweet girl, and a strong woman. She'd make Jacob a good wife.

Playing at being completely off her rocker was easier than she'd imagined. And more fun. Maybe it was a little bit mean, but desperate times called for desperate measures. Jacob hadn't been home in five years. Five years! And that time he'd flown into Atlanta one day and out the next, barely home long enough to say hello to his immediate family. Family was important. Family was everything!

Only one of her four grandsons—Ben, who had not chosen wisely—was married. Caleb and Luke were both older than Jacob, and neither of them had married. Well, Caleb had tried when he'd been a younger man, but she'd had cheese last longer than that marriage. She'd deal with the other two soon enough, but the situation with Jacob was critical.

No one knew it, except for Lurlene and Doc Porter, but Eunice had become quite good at browsing the internet with her laptop computer. The family thought she used the laptop for playing solitaire, and sometimes she did. But when no one was watching she browsed the internet with the best of them. A few weeks ago she'd run across an alarming photo that had sent warning bells off in her head. Jacob, at some highfalutin event, a skinny brunette in a tiny black dress clinging to his arm...

If she didn't do something he would marry a woman just like the one in the picture. Maybe not her, exactly, but someone like her. Shallow. Bony. Caring about nothing but money and possessions. They'd have one or two spoiled kids who'd grow up to be totally worthless, and she'd be lucky to see Jacob again before she passed even if she lived to be a hundred and twenty.

He'd lost his way. It was up to her to help him find his way back again. Daisy Bell was a big part of the plan. Eunice didn't believe for a minute that they weren't still in love.

All she had to do was remind them of that fact. She had two and a half weeks to get it done.

"Try it on," she instructed. Eunice looked at Susan and Madison. She narrowed her eyes, squinting at Madison. "Who are you? Are you the seamstress? I thought Lurlene could handle any alterations, but Susan, if you think it's best that we hire someone..."

Madison's lips narrowed. "Grandma Eunice, it's me, Maddy. I'm married to Ben, remember? We've been married almost two years."

Eunice had practiced her confused expression in the mirror countless times, and she called upon it now. Her eyes widened and she blinked fast several times. She puckered her mouth, very slightly before saying, "Ben isn't married! Why, he's much too young." Seven years ago, when Jacob and Daisy had been together, Ben hadn't been married. He hadn't even known this whiny girl. Oh, if only she really could turn back the clock.

Eunice didn't like Ben's wife much. The girl didn't dress properly, wore too much makeup, didn't go to church every Sunday and couldn't carry on an intelligent conversation to save her life. The last thing she'd read had probably been the side of a cereal box.

But Daisy...Daisy was sharp as a tack. She had her priorities straight. She went to church every Sunday, and that was a plus even if she was a Methodist. She'd sacrificed for her family, and that made her the kind of woman Jacob needed. And fast.

Eunice reminded herself, not for the first time, not to get too carried away. If she seemed to have really lost it, they might decide to lock her away somewhere, or the doctors they'd threatened to call in would show up long before the reunion—and the wedding. She needed to appear to be just a little bit crazy, not entirely cuckoo.

One way or another, she *would* get what she wanted.

Madison stormed out of the room, near tears. Daisy stared after her. Poor girl. She was so upset about Eunice's condition.

Daisy carefully placed the gown across Eunice's bed. It was so old she was afraid to touch it, much less try it on! The satin was a soft ivory, and the cut of the gown was surprisingly sleek and simple.

"I want to see it on you, dear," Eunice said in a voice that held not a hint of dementia. She was matriarch of this family, and was accustomed to being obeyed. Always.

If the old woman hadn't been sick, Daisy never would've agreed to try on the wedding gown. It was painful, to be reminded of what she'd never have. It hurt, to have the past brought back in such a sharp, detailed way. She and

Jacob were never going to get married. Those "Mrs. Daisy Tasker" doodles were ancient history. All the plans they'd made, the simple dreams she'd had…gone.

She should hate this house and everyone in it. For a long time she'd been so sure that these people would one day be her family, that the house would one day be her family home as well as Jacob's. It hurt…but she couldn't hate the house or the people. No, it couldn't be that easy.

Daisy caressed the fabric then pulled her hand back, afraid the simple touch might damage the satin. "I can't do it," she whispered, and then she looked up. Jacob's mother and grandmother were both staring at her. She tried to smile. "I'm sorry. I simply ate too much for supper. I'm not accustomed to Lurlene's cooking, and I just know I'm two sizes bigger than I was when I sat down to dinner. Tomorrow?" she offered. "I can come by after I close the shop and try on the gown."

She half expected an argument from Miss Eunice, but Jacob's grandmother smiled sweetly. "Of course. You must come for supper again tomorrow night. I've already asked Lurlene to make chicken and dumplings. Oh, and you know what I'm in the mood for? Your dear, sweet mother's lemon cake. Bless her soul. She used to bring it to the annual Fourth of July picnic and I always looked forward to eating a big piece. Sweet and tangy and rich… so amazingly *rich*. Do you have the recipe?"

"I do." Not that she'd ever attempted to make that cake. It had taken her mother half a day to prepare!

"Lovely. Tomorrow night, chicken and dumplings and lemon cake." It was a command that left no room for negotiation.

Daisy carefully returned the wedding gown to the wardrobe, kissed Eunice on the cheek and left the room. Once she was in the hallway, the door closed behind her, she shut her eyes and leaned against the wall. The hall was deserted, thank heavens, and she took a moment to gather her senses, as best she could. By tomorrow night Eunice would surely have forgotten about the wedding gown and the lemon cake, and Daisy could pass the evening blessedly alone, eating a frozen dinner and watching something mindless on television.

This was torture, pure and simple. Her legs were a little wobbly and her heart was beating much too hard. Daisy pushed away from the wall and headed not for the parlor where she assumed Jacob would be waiting but for the front porch. She needed a few minutes alone, a little bit of time to rein in her jumbled emotions.

She pushed the screen door open and headed for the porch swing that faced west. The days were long, in the midst of summer, and the sunsets across the expanse of Tasker land were breathtaking. This sunset was no exception. She'd seen more than a few, from this very porch swing. Normally she had not enjoyed them alone. This porch swing, Jacob, a couple glasses of iced tea, whispers, a stolen kiss or two or twenty...

Daisy sat there and vowed not to allow an old woman's fantasies to drag her into the past. She'd moved on, made a new and good life for herself. She didn't think about what might've been. Very often. Oh, hell, who was she kidding? She thought about it all the time!

And her life wasn't new at all. It was old and familiar. Bell Grove was home and she belonged here. She didn't need or *want* her life to be new and exciting.

She pushed off with a toe and swung lightly, hoping the gentle movement would soothe her jangled nerves. Having the past thrown in her face without warning forced her to look long and hard at the present. The truth of the matter was, she thought about Jacob entirely too much. That's why she hadn't had a serious relationship since they'd broken up. That's why she never had more than two dates with the same guy, why she found something wrong with every man who expressed an interest in her. She wasn't as pretty as Lily, but she wasn't exactly a troll, either. She could've had several serious relationships in the past few years, if she'd wanted to. She might even have found a man who'd make a good husband and father. And it took having Jacob right under her nose to allow her to see what she'd done.

Sitting in that porch swing alone, Daisy could see that she'd put her life on hold for a man who didn't deserve it. Where romance was concerned she was marking time, stagnant, stuck in a rut. A man was really all her life lacked. A man was the only thing Bell Grove had not been able to provide. How incredibly stupid! She couldn't give up the opportunity to build a family of her own just because her first love had disappointed her.

That's all Jacob was; her first love. Not her last, not her only. She didn't try to fool herself into thinking that she'd never loved him. She had. Deeply and completely. But that was then and this was now. Somehow her *now* had gone seriously askew. If this little charade—painful as it was—helped her to truly put Jacob in her past where he belonged, then it would be worthwhile.

He must've heard her leaving the house, because she hadn't been in the swing long before Jacob stepped onto the porch. Of course he knew just where she was. The gentle squeak of the porch swing, as she pushed herself back and forth with her toe, was a dead giveaway.

"Sorry," he said when he saw her there.

For so many things… She didn't go there. What was the point? "Not your fault." *This time.* "Bless her heart, one minute she seems just fine and the next she's completely befuddled."

"Yeah." Jacob walked toward her, and for a moment she wondered if he would sit beside her on the swing. It was more than big enough for two, but she wished, very hard, that he wouldn't make that move. She didn't want him that close; she didn't want that stark reminder of the old days.

The old days were gone, and there was no getting them back. Now all she had to do was convince herself that she didn't want them back.

He stopped a few feet away, almost as if he'd had the same thought. "I didn't know about the…the…"

"Wedding," she said briskly, providing the word he apparently could not.

"She'll forget about it." It sounded like an order, as if he thought he could sway an old woman's memory by will alone.

"And if she doesn't?"

He didn't have an answer for that question.

Daisy couldn't be too angry with Jacob, much as she wanted to. He was a career-focused, ambitious workaholic who'd let her go when keeping her had become inconvenient. He'd chosen his career over her. He hadn't loved her enough to sacrifice his grand plans for her. Family obligation had kept her here, while a job opportunity had taken him far, far away. They hadn't been able to make her need to provide a familiar home for her sisters and his desire for a new career to work together. He'd moved on, and he hadn't looked back, and she shouldn't hate him because he'd managed to do what she could not.

But he loved his grandmother and would apparently do anything to make her final days good ones. Maybe he did have a heart under that expensive suit, after all. That heart just wasn't meant for her.

"So," she said softly. "How's your life?"

He seemed surprised that she asked. "Good. Busy, but good. You?"

"Spectacular," she said, her voice low. "I like my life. I *love* my life." Maybe if she said it often enough she'd be able to gloss over the lack of romance in her almost-perfect life.

"Good."

Daisy wished she was the kind of woman who could purposely hurt someone who had hurt her. She wished she could tell Jacob how ecstatically happy she was, how active her sex life was, how she'd never wanted for a man's attention in the past seven years, how she hadn't missed him at all. But while she could lie to protect an old woman, she couldn't make herself lie to purposely cause pain.

As if he cared...

Jacob looked at Daisy as if he were seeing her for the first time. When she caught his eye he didn't turn away, didn't try to pretend that he wasn't studying her as if he could see beneath her skin. He looked at her with an intensity that was so much a part of the man she'd once loved.

"I'd forgotten," he said.

"Forgotten what?" she asked, her heart skipping a beat.

"I'd forgotten how you get to me." He looked her in the eye, shifted slightly as if suddenly uncomfortable in his own skin, though he still didn't turn away or drop his eyes. And Daisy could see what was coming so clearly it hurt. He'd get to *her;* they'd end up in bed; he'd break her heart all over again.

And she could *not* allow that to happen.

Chapter Three

Perhaps he'd made a mistake when he'd let Daisy go. He hadn't had a choice, he couldn't see how his life could've unfolded in any other way, but dammit, had he made a mistake?

This was the thought that plagued Jacob as he pulled his rental car to a stop in front of Daisy's home. He never second-guessed his decisions, never looked back and wondered.

The sooner he finished up here and got out of town, the better off he'd be.

Daisy still lived in the house she'd grown up in, a yellow cottage a mere five blocks from the shop where she worked. The house was square and wide and one-story, with a large wraparound porch complete with a pair of matching white rockers and healthy ferns. The yard was dotted with ancient trees; the branches intertwined overhead, and while he couldn't see it from here he imagined there was still a vegetable garden out back.

Her car was parked in the driveway, but instead of pulling in behind it he stopped at the curb. A concrete sidewalk ran in front of her house, and a leg of that sidewalk shot from the street to her front porch. This was a neighborhood where the residents walked, both for exercise and for more practical reasons, where they visited one another—on special occasions and sometimes for no reason at all. Both sidewalks saw a lot of wear. Or at least, they once had. He imagined that hadn't changed.

Daisy's entire life was right here, a general store, doctor's office, pharmacy—and her work—within easy walking distance, while he flew from one time zone to another on a regular basis. He was good at what he did, a whiz with numbers and an unshakable faith in his own instincts. The men he worked for trusted his instincts, too. They trusted him with billions of dollars in investments, and he hadn't let them down yet. In fact, he'd made them all lots and lots of money.

In the early days they'd called him a whiz kid. These days he was a highly valued member of a company that continued to grow, in large part thanks to him. And what had it gotten him? Insomnia. An almost nonexistent social life. And a fat bank account.

The second he stopped the car at the curb Daisy threw open the door and jumped out, as if she couldn't wait to escape. He should wave, let her go and hurry home. But instead he shut down the engine, jumped out of the car and followed her.

She glanced over her shoulder as his car door slammed. She was not happy. "What do you think you're doing?"

"Walking you to the door."

"If a man in a suit follows me around my neighbors are going to think someone is suing me for a bad haircut, or maybe the tax man is after me."

"The tax man? Really?"

"Shoo," she said, waving her fingers in his direction.

He ignored her dismissive order and took two long steps to catch up with her. "What's your problem with the suit?"

She didn't look at him. Her chin was in the air, her hair whipped as she glanced in the opposite direction. "I have no problem with what you wear. I don't care *at all* what you wear."

"Then why have you mentioned the damn suit so often?"

"It's summertime in the Deep South," she said. "Unless you're headed to church or a funeral, the suit is downright unnatural."

Daisy stopped in front of her porch steps, then spun around to face him. She was no longer trying to avoid him. No, instead she looked him in the eye, unflinching. She was stronger than he remembered. Tougher. "On second thought, wear a suit every day for all I care. It will serve as a constant reminder that you don't belong here."

"I don't need a constant reminder that I don't belong here." No, he'd felt it every second of every day.

"Neither do I." She took a step back and up, onto the bottom step.

Jacob matched her step, moving forward but not up. He wasn't ready to let her move away. They were nose to nose, now, eye to eye. "Then who am I supposed to be reminding?"

"I don't know and I don't care."

"You're not making any sense at all...."

"I don't have to make sense if I don't want to."

Jacob shook his head. "When did we start arguing?"

"Seven years ago," Daisy snapped.

Jacob reached out, took her face in his hands, stepped into her space and kissed her. He wasn't sure why, he just couldn't help himself. He had to kiss her; he had to press his mouth to hers. He'd thought her scent was maddening, but her taste…he had forgotten…how the hell had he forgotten this…

She tensed for a moment then she melted. Her lips molded to his, her eyes closed and they kissed. Long and soft and easy.

He never should've let her go.

She tasted so good, so warm and right. Her face in his hands was soft, and he loved holding her almost as much as he loved kissing her. She kissed him back, well and deeply. She leaned toward him, into him and when he swept his tongue just inside her mouth she gasped and moaned and deepened the kiss. The years melted away, the miles that had come between them no longer mattered.

Daisy pulled away from him sharply. Her lips were swollen and wet, her eyes wide and surprised. Was she surprised by the kiss, or by her response?

"Don't do that again," she ordered, backing up the front porch steps, toward the front door and escape.

"Why not?"

"Because it's a very bad idea."

He didn't follow her onto the porch; he'd pushed his luck enough for one day.

"Tomorrow night," he reminded her. "Lemon cake and chicken and dumplings."

"Surely Miss Eunice will forget all about those plans by tomorrow morning," Daisy said as she stopped by the front door and grabbed her house keys out of her small purse. "I hope," she added beneath her breath.

"If she doesn't…"

"She *will,*" Daisy said, almost as if she was commanding it to be so.

"Maybe. Probably." Jacob stood on the walk for several minutes after Daisy had closed the front door. When he'd heard about his grandmother's condition and decided to come home for a long visit, he hadn't expected this. He hadn't expected to have the past come to life again, to look at Daisy and suffer a deep regret for what he'd lost.

He shook his head, as if he could shake off unwanted thoughts, and turned around sharply to make his escape. Coming home had been a mistake. He'd had his reasons, and it was too late to turn back now. But the truth of the matter was, his life was no longer here in Bell Grove. It hadn't been for a very long time. Daisy and the reactions she elicited were a part of another life, and no matter how pleasant—and frustrating—it was to see her again, he had to remember to leave her in the past. Where she belonged.

Daisy didn't think she'd be able to sleep, after everything that had happened in the past twenty hours, but after Jacob dropped her at home she slept amazingly well. She dreamed about the kiss, which was very annoying because in her dream that kiss didn't end too soon. In her dream she got a lot more than a kiss from Jacob. She woke with a start, sweating and shaking and most of all angry with herself for allowing her badly neglected physical needs to wipe away every ounce of common sense. First the kiss, then the dream. Where was her self-control? Why couldn't she just be angry with him and leave it at that?

She should've bolted when he'd moved in for a kiss. She could have. Should have. But she'd wanted that kiss so much, and at that moment the want had been a lot stronger than her sense of what she *should* do.

Her dad had always been philosophical. Everything happened for a reason, he'd said on numerous occasions. There was a purpose in every heartbreak, in every decision, in every coincidence. She'd dismissed that way of thinking for a long time, because she hadn't been able to believe that her parents had died for some lofty reason that she didn't understand.

But as she walked to work she convinced herself that Jacob had returned to Bell Grove for a specific purpose, that Miss Eunice had lost her mind to put Daisy in this very position. Why? Easy. So she could get over Jacob once and for all and move on with her life.

They'd never had it out, had never really ended their relationship. They'd simply drifted apart, fallen into lives so different there was just no way to make them mesh. If she ever wanted to move on she had to get over Jacob, once and for all. Oh, she'd insisted to anyone who would listen that she'd gotten over him years ago, she'd even convinced herself, for a while. But now she knew that was a lie. If she'd really gotten over him, the unfortunate kiss wouldn't have affected her the way it had. Looking at Miss Eunice's wedding dress wouldn't have given her shivers. As well as a bout of unexpected nausea, if she were being completely honest.

She should have a few days to come up with a plan. As bad as her memory was these days, Miss Eunice had surely already forgotten about chicken and dumplings and lemon cake. What were the odds that she'd also forget that her grandson and Daisy were "engaged"? Daisy could hope, but the engagement seemed to be a thing Miss Eunice had grabbed on to, and she likely wasn't going to let it go easily. There was such joy on her face as she planned a wedding that would never take place.

Jacob seemed to think he was humoring his grandmother by playing along—and by dragging Daisy into the family mess—but what would happen if Miss Eunice's fantasy didn't fade? Did he really expect that she would go through with a fake wedding ceremony at his family reunion? No, something had to break before that happened. This charade couldn't go any further.

Much as she wanted to get Jacob out of her heart once and for all, Daisy knew very well that pretending to be his *wife* would shatter that heart beyond saving.

The morning was an easy one, until her eleven o'clock cut and color started talking about Jacob. She supposed it was inevitable that everyone would find out he was back, but you'd think people would have better manners! Not Amanda Williams, who had never met a silent moment she liked.

She started while Daisy was applying color to her hair.

"I hear Jacob Tasker is in town."

Daisy made a noncommittal humming noise that sounded affirmative enough to her.

"I also heard that he was in your shop yesterday. Did he need a haircut or did he just stop by to chat? I'm sure none of the Taskers handles their own engine repair—they have people for that sort of thing. And really, why on earth would he want someone from Bell Grove to cut his hair?" She laughed, not realizing that she'd just insulted Daisy— Daisy, who had scissors and a variety of interesting hair dyes within reach. "Oh, you two were *such* a cute couple, back in the old days." She barely took a breath, much less leave spaces in the conversation for Daisy to actually respond. Which was just as well, in Daisy's opinion.

"Everyone always knew Jacob would light out of town as soon as he got the chance. He was always so smart, so driven to succeed. I didn't think he'd go without you, though."

Well, he did. Daisy wondered if it was too late to add some purple to the color she was putting on Amanda's honey-blond hair. Maybe a Mohawk...

"I hear he looks good. Is he married, do you know? Still

working for that same company that hired him right out of college? I haven't heard much about him for a couple of years, but that doesn't mean anything."

He looks damn good, I don't know for certain if he's married or not but I don't think so and last time I checked he was still working for that soulless money-hungry company that stole him out from under me. "I need you to sit under the dryer, now," Daisy said.

Sadly the noise of the dryer didn't shut Amanda up. She raised her voice and continued, thankfully moving on to the other Taskers. Sure, a beauty shop was a great place to gossip, but Amanda's rambling made Daisy wonder what the residents of Bell Grove had been saying about her lately. All gossip concerning Daisy Bell probably began with "That poor girl, bless her heart..."

She didn't want to be a poor girl, didn't want people to bless her heart behind her back. What the hell had she done to herself? Mari and Lily didn't need her anymore. Well, they needed her as a sister and she'd always be there for them, but her years as guardian were behind her. She loved Bell Grove, loved her job and her friends, but she no longer had her sisters as a barrier keeping her from pursuing romance. Maybe there wasn't exactly a glut of handsome, available, appealing men in town, but not every man in the county was an ogre or a jerk. Why was she alone after all this time?

Jacob's return was making her question everything! Just what she didn't need: a man to screw with her head.

But she did need a man in her life. That was becoming clear. She wanted to be kissed, wanted to have sex outside of a dream, wanted to marry and have kids and make a life for herself. Maybe that would happen here in Bell Grove, and maybe it would have to happen somewhere else. She should make more trips to Atlanta, broaden her horizons.

But it wouldn't happen at all until she ended things with Jacob once and for all and allowed herself to start over.

Jacob left his grandmother's room with a frown on his face. Great. Just great! Her memory issues were pretty damn selective. And inconvenient. She had told Lurlene to prepare chicken and dumplings for supper, and she'd already started talking about how much she was looking forward to Daisy's lemon cake.

Daisy couldn't cook. She was good at a lot of things, but cooking wasn't one of them. Maybe he could drive to Atlanta and buy a lemon cake. Not that a store-bought cake, even a spectacular one, would fool Grandma Eunice even on her worst day.

It had been seven years since he'd been with Daisy, and in that time she'd raised her sisters, taken over the family business, basically grown up. Maybe she'd learned how to cook. Maybe she *did* know how to make that lemon cake. He called the shop, and she answered with a sharp,

"Bell's."

"It's me," he said.

"Me? I'm afraid you'll have to be more specific, sir." Her voice was sweeter, now, a little lower and calmer, but with an edge he couldn't dismiss. "Would you like to make an appointment for a haircut? I do have an opening this afternoon."

"Dammit, Daisy, it's *Jacob*."

"Oh, so sorry." She didn't sound sorry at all. "I didn't recognize your voice. You sounded a little bit like Old Man Johnson, but I was afraid to assume..."

"We need a lemon cake," he snapped, without arguing that he sounded nothing like Old Man Johnson, who was ninety-seven years old and had the deepest Southern drawl of any man for miles.

The moment of silence told him Daisy was as bothered as he was. "She didn't forget?"

"No. You're expected for supper, and you're expected to bring a lemon cake. She's been talking about it all morning."

"I'll call you back in fifteen minutes," she said. "I have a customer." She disconnected without a goodbye, and for a few seconds Jacob stood there with the phone in his hand, staring at it as if somehow Daisy was still there, harassing him. Driving him crazy.

Making him pay.

He hadn't purposely left her behind, it had just happened. Like that made a difference. He'd planned to send for her, to send for them all, but the one time he'd mentioned moving, Daisy had been horrified. She wouldn't uproot her sisters, she'd said, wouldn't drag them away from their friends and the only home they'd ever known. He'd planned to come home for Christmas that year, to convince her face-to-face to return to California with him.

But he hadn't made Christmas that year. There had been a business emergency—in hindsight so unimportant that right now he could not remember what it had been—and he'd canceled his travel plans.

And that had been that, though there had been a few awkward phone conversations in the early months of the new year. Not many and nothing had been said that could break through the distance between them, distance both physical and emotional. He and Daisy had no longer wanted the same things. They'd drifted apart. His life was there, her life was here. Simple. She'd faded in his memory, as he was certain he'd faded in hers. Life went on.

Dammit, that hadn't been entirely his fault. She'd played a part, as well. Maybe he hadn't fought for her the way he should have, but she hadn't exactly fought for him, either.

When Daisy called back he was still holding the cordless phone in his hand, ready for her. Her words were sharp. "Grab a pen and paper. I'm going to tell you what I need, and you're going to put on that fancy suit of yours and head to the Piggly Wiggly."

A part of her wanted to kick Jacob out of her house and tackle this chore alone, but two things stopped her. One, she needed the help. Two, she'd never get over him if she didn't kick this annoying habit of being downright twitchy when he was around. Not twitchy in a bad way. No, he made her squirm in a way that was annoyingly pleasant. She felt like he had literally worked his way under her skin.

He looked good in khakis and a golf shirt. She'd kidded him about his suits, but he did look sharp in them. The more casual outfit he wore this afternoon showed off the muscle he'd built up since he'd left her. Not massive muscle, thank goodness, but he did have some interesting definition.

More reminder that they weren't the same people they'd been seven years ago. Of course they weren't! They'd been little more than babies, untouched by the real world, unshaped by loss and hardship and responsibility.

Daisy tried to keep her mind on lemon cake, but she really wanted to touch Jacob's forearm to see if it felt as hard as it looked. She wanted to look under that shirt—just a peek—to see what muscles he'd added there. He'd probably added some chest hair, as well. He hadn't had much at twenty-four. Oh, she really hoped he hadn't turned into one of those guys who worked out in a gym and waxed his chest....

Her mind could not wander there.

"Do you actually play golf?" she asked, pointing at

the dark blue shirt with the little embroidered doodad on the pocket.

"No."

"Doesn't that make your outfit false advertising?"

He'd didn't answer, but he did give her a frustrated look that made her smile as he unpacked everything he'd bought at the Piggly Wiggly down the road, a small grocery store that served the next town over as well as two communities that were too small to support their own. His purchases lined the counter in the Bell kitchen, a boxy room with a small table that was older than she was and appliances that weren't much newer. They worked. And it wasn't like she cooked all that often anyway.

He picked up a box. "I'm pretty sure your mom's famous homemade lemon cake didn't start with a cake mix."

Daisy shot him a cutting glance. "No, but I don't have time to make a homemade cake, and besides, it's the icing that makes it special."

"It's a good thing you were free this afternoon."

She glared at him. Again. Still. "I wasn't *free*. I had to reschedule a regular for tomorrow afternoon. Remember Miss Hattie?"

"How could I forget. Did you tell her why you had to cancel?"

"No, I lied and told her I didn't feel well. Do you know how much I hate lying to my clients?" She didn't point out that she hated the idea that the facts of this charade might get out much more than she hated fibbing to her customers.

"Sorry. I'll be happy to pay you for any income you lose because you're helping me."

"I still don't want your money, Tasker." She made sure she sounded sharp and certain. And annoyed.

He sounded pretty annoyed, himself. "I don't want you

to lose money because you're helping me out of a tough spot."

"I'm not helping you. I'm helping your grandmother." He could drown in his *tough spots* for all she cared.

"Sorry," he said sharply. "I forgot."

The tension in the air was almost unbearable. It hung between them, like every unspoken word that haunted her, still. He was angry. She was antsy.

"Are you married?" She'd planned to ask, needed to know, but the question could've come at a better time and been delivered more graciously. Instead she'd just blurted it out, standing in the kitchen with an apron worn over a pair of denim shorts and an old red tank—she always made such a mess when she did try to cook—feet bare, a box of butter in one hand and a sack of lemons in the other. The question did diffuse the tension, a bit. Maybe because it apparently took Jacob by surprise.

He shook his head. "No."

His answer was sadly insufficient, so Daisy pressed on. "Engaged? Dating seriously? Involved with any woman on any level?"

"No."

"Why the hell not? I'm sure you're quite the catch, even in California. I'll bet the women *looooove* your Southern accent."

"I lost my Southern accent years ago," he insisted.

Daisy laughed. "Yeah, keep telling yourself that."

Jacob's lips thinned. His jaw twitched. Finally he asked, "Would I have kissed you last night if I was married, engaged, or involved?"

"Maybe," she said sharply. "Some men don't seem to have a problem with that sort of thing…they don't find it a conflict of interest at all."

"I'm not one of those men. You should know that."

She should, but it had been so long. She didn't know him at all, not really. How much had he changed? Her task of kicking him out of her head and her heart would be so much easier if he'd turned into a jerk.

"So, there's no significant other waiting for you on the other side of the country, no woman sitting at home alone, waiting for your phone calls," she said calmly. "I can't help but wonder, why not?"

Daisy wanted, more than anything, for Jacob to convince her that he didn't deserve to visit her dreams and send her well-ordered life spinning out of control. The boy she'd once loved was gone. What kind of man had he become?

She studied him, up and down. *Be a complete ass, please. That will make this so much easier.*

Chapter Four

Why not? *No time, no inclination.* He'd dated, but never the same girl more than twice. Jacob hadn't questioned that MO until Daisy had come back into his life, however temporarily.

He was forced to consider that the reason he'd never met a woman who really did it for him wasn't because he worked so many hours, wasn't because he was so focused on his career that he didn't have the time for a serious relationship. Maybe the sad truth was that no one else had ever affected him this way because no one else was Daisy.

"Can we just make a cake?" he snapped.

Daisy switched on the oven, collected a large bowl and a small pot from a lower cabinet and then she turned to face him. "Sorry to pry. Amanda asked today if you were married, and I was horrified to realize that I didn't know."

Because he'd kissed her, and she'd kissed him back, and Daisy Bell would never have knowingly kissed a married man that way. "What about you?" He'd know if she was married. Someone would've told him, he supposed, and if she was married this charade never would've gotten off the ground, but... "Are you seeing anyone? Is there a boyfriend I should be on the lookout for?"

"Not at the moment," she said coolly.

Jacob found he was sharply relieved to know that there wasn't another man in Daisy's life. He also wondered about the qualifier. Not at the moment? Who had she dated in the past? Had any of those relationships been serious? A surge of jealousy almost knocked him on his ass.

No, not jealousy. Envy. He had no right to be jealous. He'd had his shot and he'd blown it. He wanted Daisy to be happy, to have everything she wanted and needed. At the same time, he couldn't say he'd be happy to see her with another man.

It annoyed him to realize that in spite of all the obstacles, he wanted Daisy again. While he was here, while they were forced to endure one another's company...he wanted her. The certainty of that wanting hit him low in the gut, as they worked together in her warm, cozy kitchen. His presence here, in her kitchen, wasn't really necessary, but he didn't back away, didn't come up with an excuse to bolt. He fetched things for her. He washed and dried bowls, and he moved out of her way when she started to dance from one counter to another, from the sink to the stove to the counter. His mind was *not* on cake.

He wanted to kiss Daisy again, but this time he wouldn't stop. He wanted to make love to her. He wanted to watch her laugh in bed, wanted to dance with her, naked, the way they once had. More than reliving old memories, he wanted to make new ones. With her.

He was old enough now to understand why she hadn't been able to come to him. She'd done what she had to do, what she'd believed to be best for her family. Maybe in hindsight she understood, too, why he hadn't been able to stay here. They couldn't go back and undo what had been done, but that didn't mean they couldn't forget that pain and get to know one another all over again.

He wanted her, Daisy the woman, Daisy who had said she wouldn't kiss him again, Daisy who occasionally looked at him as if she was willing him to disappear.

Jacob wasn't afraid of a challenge. Never had been. In fact, he loved a challenge more than just about anything.

Daisy licked a dollop of icing off the tip of her finger. The cake looked a little rubbery—maybe it had cooked too long—but the icing was awesome. How could it not be? Confectioners sugar, butter, lemon juice, whole milk. It was the icing that made the cake, anyway. Maybe Miss Eunice wouldn't remember exactly how the lemon cake used to taste. Maybe fabulous icing alone would be enough. She could hope!

"My turn." Jacob leaned in, looked down on the pot that had bits of icing clinging to the sides and waited.

"Go ahead," she said, starting to back away. He was too close for comfort. Just having him so near made her skin itch as if it was resizing itself to fit over her body. But before she could move away, he placed a hand at the small of her back. That hand was firm, warm and steady. It held her in place without undue pressure. It grounded her. Her entire body seemed to thump, as if the earth had just shifted in a major way. She had never before been so keenly aware of a *touch*. She could move away, she could simply step to the side and that hand would fall. She didn't move. If anything, she shifted slightly closer to Jacob.

He put his other hand over hers, guided both into the pot, scooped a bit of icing from the side of the pot onto *her* finger and lifted it to his mouth. He wasn't going to… he wouldn't dare…

He did. Jacob placed her finger in his mouth and sucked. No part of the act, not even the sucking, was hard or violent or forceful; his touch was actually very light. Easy. Just west of casual. Again, she could've stopped him, could've moved her hand away, but *again* she didn't. Instead she watched his mouth close over her finger, felt the warm, moist flick of his tongue.

If she'd felt that touch only on her finger she'd be all right, but no—she felt the way Jacob touched her in her entire body, from the top of her head to her curling toes. She felt it in her scalp, in her breasts, between her legs. She took the opportunity to place her free hand on his forearm. Yep, hard as rock and wonderfully warm to the touch. If she had even a tiny bit less self-control, she'd throw him on the floor and strip him naked and have her way with him here and now.

She was still curious about his current chest hair situation.

Thankfully she *did* have some self-control. And dignity. Both were fading fast, though. "I told you…"

Jacob slowly pulled her finger from his mouth. "You said no kissing. You didn't say a word about licking icing off your finger."

"Do I have to be *that* specific?" She dropped her hand, but didn't back away. She'd never admit it, at least not aloud, but she liked having him so close she could see the stubble on his jaw, see each and every hair on his forearm. She liked that she could smell him, and though he had changed and she had changed, his scent and her reaction to it remained the same. Like it or not she was drawn to Jacob the way iron was drawn to a magnet.

"I wish you would be specific," he said, his head dipped

down to bring it too close to hers. "What exactly do you not want me to do to you?"

He was teasing her, knowing damn well that she couldn't stand here and tell him not to touch her, not to make her feel itchy all over, not to invade her dreams. *Please, Jacob, don't look at me that way. Don't make me love you all over again.*

She backed away. Slowly. Reluctantly. "I have to change."

"Yes, Grandma Eunice will be shocked if you show up dressed like that. Not that I'd mind. You look amazing."

She should've worn old, baggy sweats instead of shorts and a tank, no matter how warm it was in the kitchen. Too much skin was exposed, and the way Jacob was staring at her...

She had to throw up a barrier between them, had to re-mind him—and herself—why they didn't work. "Too bad I don't have tennis whites or a matching golf shirt and a skort to wear. Wouldn't we make a fine preppy couple."

He didn't have a snappy comeback for that one. No, he just looked confused. "What's a skort?"

"Half skirt, half shorts. Skort."

It annoyed him when she criticized the way he dressed, she noticed. Funny. She didn't remember him caring much about such things in the old days. No, he'd cared about his grades, his plans for the future and her. He'd played guitar—as badly as she sang along—and he'd worked on old cars. He and Caleb had always had a project in the separate garage behind Tasker House, but these days she supposed he'd have a conniption if he wound up with grease under his fingernails. He'd been a whiz with the cars, but he'd never been able to master playing the guitar. He did everything else so well, he didn't fail at anything. Except playing the guitar. And keeping her.

These days he cared about clothes and work. That seemed like a huge step backward to her.

Daisy left Jacob in the kitchen while she all but ran to her bedroom to change clothes. She reached into her closet with a specific outfit in mind. Lavender slacks, matching blouse, strappy sandals. Too bad she didn't have a chastity belt in her closet, somewhere. She needed something to remind her why she couldn't have what she really wanted. Iron, lock and key...not a bad idea...

With her hand on the lavender outfit, another idea popped into her head. A *brilliant* idea, if she did say so herself.

She was in this uncomfortable situation for Miss Eunice's sake, not for Jacob's, not for any of the other Taskers. For some reason, Miss Eunice not only thought she and Jacob were engaged, she approved. Heartily. But she didn't approve of Ben's wife, Maddy. Not at all. She obviously didn't like the way Maddy dressed, spoke, or wore her makeup and hair. Maybe Maddy was a bit flashy and flamboyant, but everyone was entitled to their own style. Maddy's style was just kind of slutty, bless her heart.

Daisy let her hand fall. She stood at the open closet for a moment and asked herself...What would happen if Miss Eunice didn't approve of *her?* The wedding wouldn't seem so attractive and pressing, then. Daisy didn't want to shock Miss Eunice, didn't want to send the old woman into a conniption fit or anything, but if she started to disapprove of the match, even just a little bit...

Daisy closed her closet door, peeked into the hallway and jetted across to Lily's old room, a wide smile on her face. For the first time all day she felt as if she were in control. Not Miss Eunice, not Jacob, not her traitorous body. She was going to put an end to this debacle, once and for all.

* * *

She was trying to kill him. That was the only explanation.

At first, Daisy had insisted on driving herself to the house for dinner, but Jacob had talked her into riding with him again. He wanted her close; he wanted to steal glimpses of her as he drove down the deserted road between downtown Bell Grove and Tasker House. He wanted her in his presence for as long as possible; he wanted to be able to reach out and touch her, even if he didn't.

He wasn't sure why she'd eventually given in and agreed to make the short trip with him, in his rental car, he was just glad for it. She sat in the passenger seat, the lemon cake in her lap, her long, tanned, bare legs stretching out beyond the pale yellow, slightly lopsided dessert.

He'd like to think that maybe, just maybe, she'd agreed to come along for the same reasons he'd wanted her here. Did she like being near him, even just a little? Her words were sharp, and she'd given no sign—beyond her instinctive response to the kiss and his mouth on her finger—that she had any romantic feelings left for him. Still, he could hope. She'd never admit it, but chemistry like this couldn't be one-sided.

Jacob kept his attention entirely on the road for a few minutes. That final thought made him sound like a stalker. Like it or not, it was entirely possible that what he felt for her *was* one-sided.

But he didn't think that was the case.

When Daisy had stepped into the kitchen—after what seemed like an awfully long time to change clothes—she'd been transformed. She wore a floral print dress with a flirty skirt that was *very* short and a V-neck that was *very* deep. The four inch heels made her already long legs look incredibly long. Her hair was piled on top of her head in an artfully messy way, and she wore more makeup than he'd ever seen on her pretty face.

She was all boobs and legs and red lipstick. And what fine boobs and legs they were.

"You're a little overdressed for chicken and dumplings," he'd argued.

"Look who's talking about being overdressed," she'd countered.

Neither of them had said a word as he drove the final mile toward Tasker House. Daisy was up to something, he just didn't know what. Was she rubbing every gorgeous attribute she possessed in his face in order to torture him? If so, her plan was working. He was definitely tortured.

He pulled into a parking space close to the porch and shut off the engine of his rental car. Daisy—who was usually annoyingly independent—sat in the car and waited for him to round it and open her door. When he did so she offered him the cake. He laughed. She hadn't simply been waiting for him to open her door like a gentleman; she wasn't able to exit the car in those shoes with a layer cake in her hands. He took the cake from her, and watched as she grabbed her little purse and very carefully peeled herself out of the car. Slowly. Gracefully. *Damn*. His mouth went dry.

"What are you up to?" he asked as they approached the front door. He carried the cake, so his hands were full. Just as well.

"I have no idea what you're talking about," she said sweetly, and then she stumbled. As she recovered she tugged her skirt down as much as was possible. Which wasn't much. She wasn't accustomed to walking in those high heels, any more than she was used to a skirt that barely covered her butt. No, this was a show of some sort. She was in costume. For his benefit? He wasn't sure. What kind of woman told a man to keep his distance then turned up wearing a dress like that one?

As if he could understand how a woman thought.

Inside the house, he handed the cake over to Lurlene, whose eyes widened when she saw Daisy. Daisy dropped her purse on an entryway table and took a moment to once again adjust her teeny skirt. She twisted her body, as if she could realign her hips to make the skirt a bit longer. It didn't work. The cook who had been with the Taskers since before Jacob was born didn't say a word, not right away, but she walked toward the kitchen with the cake in her hands, shaking her head and mumbling something under her breath when she was too far away for them to make out the words.

Jacob and Daisy walked toward the parlor. Slowly, since she was unable to walk any other way in those heels. She pulled on the skirt again, and then adjusted the flimsy fabric that barely covered her breasts.

Again he asked. "What are you up to with that getup?"

"How do you know I don't dress like this all the time, these days?"

He didn't, so he kept his mouth shut.

"This is supposed to be a date, after all. I'm not a child anymore, Jacob, I'm all grown up. I'm certainly not the same naive girl I was when we dated. I've changed, I've matured." She lifted her chin and rotated her head slowly to look at him with ice-cold blue eyes.

They reached the parlor before he could respond, which was just as well since he had no idea what to say. The idea of Daisy dressing like this for another man was more than he could handle, even though he knew, logically, that he had no right to care how she dressed or for whom. Logic flew out the window where Daisy was concerned.

He found himself wondering who she'd dated, who she'd worn that dress for, who she'd kissed on the front porch....

As soon as he entered the room and saw Maddy pouting on the love seat by the bookcase, her own long legs displayed beyond a very short skirt, her own high heeled shoes dangling from her feet, he understood Daisy's motives in a flash that momentarily stopped him in his tracks. He should've realized immediately what she was up to. He turned to Daisy, narrowed his eyes and whispered, "Really?"

She just smiled back and walked into the room with confidence, those long legs and a nice swell of full breasts out there for everyone to see. The shock was evident on every face as they took in her new style. Even Grandma Eunice's face displayed disapproval and surprise. Ben's tongue was practically hanging out. His mom's eyes widened and she took a step back. His dad narrowed his gaze, squinting in Daisy's direction as if he couldn't believe what he was seeing. Jacob wouldn't have been surprised if his dad literally hit the floor.

Maddy didn't get it at all. She was completely oblivious to the reactions around her as she smiled widely, straightened her spine and said, "Oh, I love that dress."

Grandma Eunice muttered beneath her breath, "Of course you do."

Okay, so it wasn't the best idea she'd ever had. Her feet hurt, she could feel the blister on the big toe of her right foot taking shape and she was already tired of Ben checking out her cleavage every time he got the chance. He wasn't even bothering to be subtle about it! They weren't halfway through the meal, and Daisy already regretted her impulsive decision to take her cue from Maddy Tasker.

She needed to have a long, big sister talk with Lily. This

dress should never come out of the closet again! And the shoes, how did Lily walk in these things? Surely she didn't dress like this for her new job, or for dating in Atlanta, or for, well, anything.

Even worse, her plan hadn't worked. At all. Miss Eunice was still talking about the wedding. She hadn't mentioned the scandalous dress or the makeup or the shoes, not once. She repeated herself often, but she never veered from her purpose. At this rate there would be a wedding at the Tasker Reunion whether she and Jacob agreed to it or not. Miss Eunice would probably sit there in her wheelchair, front and center, shouting at the top of her lungs, "They do! They do!"

Would that be legal? Surely not, but if Miss Eunice could find a way to make it legal, she would.

The Tasker Reunion seemed very far away, at the moment. It was only one issue in a mountain of problems Daisy faced. For now, she needed to focus on surviving this night.

It wasn't going to be easy.

Jacob, having figured out her plan, was making her pay for her foolishness. He sat to her left, and one hand had found its way to her thigh not long after they'd taken their chairs. For a while that hand had just rested there, warm and heavy, and then, about the time she attempted to take a bite of the chicken and dumplings, that hand began to move. Not a lot, but it was movement, his fingers brushing against her bare leg. She'd jumped in response, once, then shooed at a nonexistent fly to explain away her twitch.

That hand was still on her thigh. It was warm, and heavy, and large. The fingers molded to the shape of her leg, brushing her inner thigh. She couldn't eat, not with Jacob's hand resting on her thigh as if it belonged there. A boulder had settled in her throat, so she didn't even try to take another bite. She reached down, put her hand over his, lifted it and placed that hand on his own thigh. Ten seconds later, the hand was back. Higher this time.

Like it or not, her body responded to Jacob's touch. Her body remembered, and long-neglected nerve endings danced just because his skin rested against hers. She wanted to throw that hand off her leg and move as far away from Jacob as possible. But she didn't want to make a scene at the table. Miss Eunice wouldn't understand why Daisy wouldn't allow her "fiancé" to touch her.

The dinner plates were cleared away, and the lemon cake was deposited on the table. Daisy hadn't been able to swallow more than three bites of chicken and dumplings, so she was still hungry. Unfortunately her throat was about to close up and she wasn't sure she could swallow. One finger on the hand at her thigh began to rock back and forth, every sway taking it higher and firmer and closer to her center. Like it or not, she throbbed. Like it or not, she *wanted* Jacob to touch her there.

Muscle memory, she told herself, that's all it was. When they'd been together, the sex had been great. No other man could make her feel that way, could make her lose control and scream and laugh and shudder.

Not that she'd ever given another man the chance…

Everyone seemed to enjoy the cake, but her. She looked at the piece on her plate, lifted a glob of icing onto her finger and licked it off. That was it. She couldn't swallow another bite.

Jacob seemed to be enjoying his cake well enough, taking big bites, complimenting her as everyone else did. If anyone had figured out she'd used a cake mix instead of her mother's old recipe, they were too polite to mention it. How dare he smile and act as if everything was right in his world? How dare he sit there, with his hand up her skirt, and act as if nothing was going on beneath the table?

Almost too late, the shock wore off and Daisy decided two could play his game. She'd decided to take control of the situation by dressing this way and attempting to scare his grandmother into changing her mind about the wedding, and with a touch Jacob had stolen that control from her. She couldn't let him get away with that.

Beneath the table, she placed her hand on Jacob's thigh. High, firm, familiar. Her fingertips moved, just a little. He almost choked on his last bite of cake when she stroked, allowing her hand to travel higher than was proper. But they were "engaged," after all. For all intents and purposes, they were a couple. She let her hand slide to his inner thigh. To his credit, he didn't jump out of his chair. But he tensed, and his neck turned red.

How much did her touch affect him? If she let her hand travel higher, would she find further evidence of his reaction? She wasn't brave enough to check, but the slight tremble she felt in his thigh gave her a good indication that he was not unaffected.

Good. She wasn't the only one vulnerable to this kind of torture.

Instead of being properly chastised and realizing—with regret—what he'd been doing to her throughout the meal, Jacob recovered and retaliated. His hand squeezed her thigh then it moved boldly higher. Slowly, firmly. Full of talent and promise and memory. Daisy couldn't breathe. The room got small and too warm, and someone was speaking but she couldn't make out the words. Her knees were all but knocking, her skin grew overly warm. His hand, big and warm and assured, slipped so far beneath her short skirt he was *right there*. Her thighs fell apart, just slightly.

Before Jacob could touch her where she ached for him, where she wanted him to touch her, Daisy pushed her chair back, broke all contact with him and excused herself from the table. She rushed from the dining room, headed for the guest bathroom down the hallway.

What had she been thinking? Why the hell was she even here? Had she really thought she could play chicken with Jacob and win?

In the small bathroom, she put down the toilet lid and plopped onto it. Pretending was exhausting. She wasn't an actress; she was a good hairdresser with enough mechanical skill to handle a simple engine repair. Acting was not her strong suit. She couldn't pretend to be someone she was not, to love someone who had hurt her. And somewhere along the way the pretending that nothing had changed had turned into full-out undeniable lust.

She wanted Jacob. She didn't love him anymore, she didn't want him to be a part of her life, she was still so mad at him that she could spit. But like it or not she wanted him in her bed. He had her aching and shaky and…dammit…needy. And really, why not? They were unattached, healthy, consenting adults. Obviously the spark that had come to life between them nine years ago was still there. And plenty strong. Why shouldn't she…why couldn't she… Oh, no, this was such a bad idea.

She had to get away from Jacob until her head cleared and her body became her own again. Maybe they could tell Miss Eunice that the bride had fallen deathly ill and the wedding was off. It was pretty clear that she wasn't going to forget about it, at least not as long as Jacob was here for her to see every day. For some reason Jacob's marriage had become a focal point for his grandmother, something she clung to while her health was deteriorating.

But Daisy knew she couldn't take this much longer. It

was torture, pure and simple. She could've lived the rest of her life without wanting Jacob Tasker this way! She'd planned to do just that, and now here she was, trembling to her marrow, throbbing, aching. And all it had taken was one stolen kiss and a hand on her thigh. Was she so easy? So desperate for affection?

"Daisy?" the tentative knock at the door was accompanied by his voice. Not Old Man Johnson's distinctive drawl, but Jacob's unforgettable voice, a voice she would remember with great clarity until the day she died. "Are you all right?"

"I'm fine. I just need a minute."

"I'm coming in."

"Good luck with that," she snapped. "I locked the..."

The cheap lock on the door popped, and Jacob walked inside. Suddenly the tiny guest bathroom was smaller than it had been before. He took up all the air in the room, all the space, and again, she couldn't breathe.

She didn't bother to stand. "Really, Jacob? What if I'd been using the facilities? Can't a girl get a little privacy around here?"

"This was a bad idea," he said, staying by the door and ignoring her questions.

"Tell me about it."

"I told everyone that you hadn't been feeling well and that I'm taking you home right away."

"No trying on my wedding dress tonight?" she asked, trying to come off cool and uncaring, instead sounding merely sad and frustrated.

"Not tonight."

Daisy stood quickly and brushed against Jacob. He caught her, held her firmly. She looked up, caught his eye, and heaven help her, she wanted to be with him here and now, in a teeny bathroom, while his family ate cake just a few yards away. She was inches away from begging him. *Please, Jacob, help me remember how good it was*. She actually scooted her body up slowly, moving her mouth closer to his, parting her lips. All rational thought was just about gone. Soon there would be nothing left but a primitive need she wouldn't be able to deny, an ache only he could satisfy.

Just about. She stopped before her lips touched his. "I need to go home."

He nodded, but didn't say a word.

"I want you to give me the keys to your car, and let me drive myself home, because I can't be with you right now."

She expected him to argue, but he surprised her. He reached into his pocket, withdrew the keys and handed them to her without a single word of argument. "Call me when you get home."

Daisy shook her head. She didn't want to talk to him, didn't want to hear his voice…didn't even want to think about him.

"If you don't, I'll show up at your house to make sure you made it home all right. Don't make me worry about you, Daisy," he added, and he sounded sincere.

She didn't want to believe he cared about her at all, didn't want to think he had a single attractive quality, beyond his obvious physical attributes. He was cold, hard, uncaring. As long as she believed that, he wouldn't be able to hurt her again.

"Fine, I'll call." If she didn't he probably would show up at her door. If he showed up at her door she'd ask him in. She'd ask him in, and she'd kiss him, and it wouldn't stop there. She wouldn't be able to help herself, and what did that say about her? How desperate was she for a man in her life when the one who'd broken her heart had her all but writhing in need?

They stepped into the hallway then moved apart. Daisy kicked off her shoes, grabbed her purse from the entry-way table and headed out the door. She didn't look back.

Eunice watched from the window for several minutes after Jacob's rental car had disappeared from view. Without Jacob in it. She bit her lip. Frowned. Drummed her fingers on the armrest of her wheelchair. Everything was *not* going according to plan. She'd been so sure that as soon as Jacob and Daisy were in the same room their love would bloom to life again. They'd been so very much in love before life and career and far too many miles had driven them apart. But apparently it was not happening as she'd planned. Otherwise Daisy wouldn't be driving home alone, and Jacob wouldn't be sitting on the front porch. Also alone.

For years her grandson had made a very good living analyzing businesses, finding their strengths and weaknesses and advising his employer on whether or not the business under scrutiny could be salvaged or should be dismantled. He had an analytical mind that allowed him to see all sides of a situation, to detach himself from emotion and find the best approach. He'd gotten that ability from her, though he likely didn't realize it. In her generation a woman hid her strengths, especially if she was considerably smarter than her husband.

It had taken Jacob some time in college to find his calling. He'd changed his major twice, early on, and had ended up spending more than four years in school. But it had been worth it. He was smart, he had honed his innate skills and now he was amazingly successful.

And he was alone.

Jacob wanted Daisy; Eunice knew that to be true. Daisy wanted him, too, even if she wouldn't admit it to herself. But the truth was, Daisy Bell was too comfortable here in Bell Grove; her roots were too deep. How could she be convinced that she was better off with Jacob than she was staying here? She would always have ties to Bell Grove, and that meant Jacob would share those ties. But having ties to a place and being rooted there were two different things entirely.

Eunice pondered the possibilities. Daisy wasn't the kind of woman who could be influenced with gifts. She could not be bought; she would not swoon over diamonds and gold. No, she was made of stronger stuff than that.

The girl was very stubborn when it came to following her heart. If she'd followed her heart she would've wound up in Jacob's arms by now, and that hadn't happened. If they'd slept together, Jacob wouldn't be wound tighter than a two-dollar watch and Daisy wouldn't have sat at the dinner table looking as if she was on the verge of literally exploding.

Stubborn young people.

As far as Eunice could see there was only one way to go. Uproot Daisy. Remove all other options. And she had to make it happen fast. This had to happen *yesterday*. She was determined that the fake wedding they were planning to patronize her wouldn't be fake at all, and that when Jacob returned to San Francisco he wouldn't be going alone.

Chapter Five

Jacob had forgotten what it was like to live in his childhood home. In San Francisco his day was tightly scheduled from the moment he woke to the late hour he fell into bed. There was no time to reflect on the choices he'd made, no quiet time where his mind wandered to dangerous—and foolish—"what might've been" territory.

It had almost killed him not to see Daisy for the past two days, but she'd made it clear that she needed time. Time was something he didn't have enough of. The clock was ticking, his time here was rushing past. He'd been so tempted to go into town just to manage a quick and "accidental" moment with her, but he hadn't. He owed her the time she'd asked for.

Preparing the Tasker property for the annual reunion meant clearing fallen limbs and cutting those which were suitable for firewood into the proper lengths to dry for the coming winter. Winters were short in Georgia, but when the occasional ice or snowstorm came through there was nothing more comforting than a wood fire in one of the many fireplaces. Unfortunately, physical labor that didn't require much in the way of actual thinking gave Jacob's mind an opportunity to wander. His mind *never* wandered. There were so many aspects of his past that he'd given little—if any—thought to until he'd come home. Family, of course. His mother was under a lot of stress; his father didn't seem to be much help. His grandmother was aging before his eyes. Ben, the youngest of the Tasker boys, had grown up. Physically he was bigger, sturdier. Mentally he was sharper, less distracted than Jacob remembered, and he seemed to be doing a good job for the family company. He still needed some maturing, but Ben was a far cry from the kid Jacob remembered. Jacob had to admit, he didn't really know his little brother anymore. Time had changed them all.

He wondered if he'd notice the same kinds of changes in Caleb and Luke, when he saw them. Of course, they hadn't been kids when Jacob had left. They'd been grown men, so the changes shouldn't be as dramatic. Still, you never knew what the years would do to a person.

Jacob had borrowed suitable work clothes from Ben, who had joined in on this hot, summer weekend to take care of the chores that had been assigned to them by their mother. She enjoyed ordering them around like they were still teenagers.

After they took care of the limbs they needed to address the fire ant hills and a wasps' nest. When that was done, Susan would give her two younger boys another list of chores. In two weeks this land would be crawling with relatives. Young and old, from near and far…the property had to be made safe. Heaven forbid that anyone might find a flaw.

Jacob hadn't been assigned chores for a very long time. He couldn't say that a day in the sun, working and thinking as little as possible, was necessarily a bad thing. Physical labor outside his usual three days at the gym proved to be invigorating and more challenging than he wanted to admit. Even if his mind did wander to unfortunate what-might've-beens.

He wouldn't allow himself to admit that he'd missed Daisy. Her smile, her eyes, her walk. The simplest things grabbed him and wouldn't let go. Not that it mattered how much she appealed to him. Even though her sisters were grown and on their own, he didn't think for a minute that Daisy would ever consider moving to San Francisco. Even if she did forgive him for not sticking with her when she'd been forced to quit college and come back home, there was the simple fact that Daisy was a small-town girl. She loved it here; she was a part of the community. This was her *home*, in every sense of the word. He'd heard it in her voice when she'd called to let him know she'd arrived home safely and told him about the neighbor girl doing cartwheels on the lawn. And when he'd spoken to her that morning and she'd mentioned stopping by the farmer's market and running into an old mutual friend, someone who'd asked about Jacob.

While he could admit to perversely enjoying his simple chores, while talking to Daisy reminded him of what it was like to truly have a home town, giving up a very lucrative career to come home and work for his mother was not an option. Tasker Enterprises was diverse and there were a dozen positions he could take, if it suited him. But no matter what he chose to do, if he was employed by Tasker Enterprises he'd be working for his mother. No, thanks.

Which left the situation with Daisy entirely unworkable. A long distance relationship hadn't worked seven years ago, and it wouldn't work now.

Ben wiped the sweat from his face, grabbed a couple cold bottles of water from the ice chest and headed Jacob's way. "Slow down, bro. The faster we get this done, the sooner we'll get new marching orders. I swear, I don't know why Mom won't hire this out. It's not like we can't afford a crew of yard men and exterminators to get this done. Why don't you convince her that she'd be assisting the local economy by hiring a couple of unemployed guys to do the grunt work?"

Jacob set his chain saw aside and took the offered water. "Either she doesn't think workmen she'd hire would do a proper job, or she just likes ordering us around like we were still kids."

Ben smiled, and for a moment he almost looked like he was no more than thirteen again, gangly and awkward. The boy was still there, barely disguised by the years. "Probably both."

"Probably." Jacob drank the water too quickly, glad for the moment of rest and the much-needed hydration.

Ben's smile faded, and he glanced toward the house as if he was afraid someone might be headed their way. "So, how's it going with Daisy?"

"How the hell do you think it's going?" Jacob snapped. "This is the worst scheme I ever agreed to participate in, and if I could take it back I would do it in a heartbeat. Daisy's miserable, I'm miserable and Grandma Eunice seems to forget about everything else *but* the wedding plans, which remain clear as a bell. I wanted to give her a few good days, I wanted to see her not so upset, but what's going to happen when the reunion rolls around and she's still set on this wedding?" Had he just made matters worse by trying to do something nice for his grandmother? Maybe he should've left well enough alone. Too late, now.

Daisy still had his rental car. He hadn't bothered to try to collect it because it wasn't like the Tasker family was lacking in modes of transportation. There was a separate four-car garage out back and every bay housed a vehicle of some sort. Besides, Daisy had been so upset when she'd left the house a couple of days ago. She seemed better on the phone, but she was still cautious where he was concerned. And the days without her slipped by.

As soon as the reunion was over, he had to get back to San Francisco and back to work. He'd been trying to keep up by cell and computer, but it wasn't the same as being there in the thick of things.

"I talked to Daisy this morning," Jacob said. "Grandma Eunice has been asking for her, so she'll be here tomorrow for lunch." He didn't mention that he'd had to gently twist her arm.

"Good! I've gotten used to seeing her on the other side of the dining room table."

Jacob stared at his little brother. "I noticed that. Stare at her boobs the way you did the last time she was here, and I'll kick your ass."

Ben laughed. "You can try." His laughter faded. "Seriously, you can ditch the macho act anytime, bro. This isn't the real thing, remember? You aren't supposed to get possessive about a woman you're not actually involved with. It's all pretend, remember?"

"Yeah, I remember," Jacob said then he gave his brother a level glare. "But that doesn't change what I said. I *will* kick your ass."

Maybe Ben was right and he had no right to feel possessive about Daisy, but that didn't do a thing to squash what he was feeling. Regret and frustration…with a little bit of unexpected hope thrown into the mix.

Mari swiped her hand back, trying to move a stubborn strand of hair out of her eyes, and ended up smearing grease across her cheek. Daisy smiled as she looked on. This was Mari's normal weekend look. Coveralls, a crooked ponytail and grease. When it came to repairing engines she was as messy in the shop as Daisy was in the kitchen.

There were some repairs Daisy could handle, but for the more complicated jobs she needed Marigold. The youngest Bell sister had always had a magic touch with engines large and small. She could've made a career of it without going to college, but she'd decided to pursue a nursing degree, instead.

Always the fixer.

"So, what's up?" Mari's eyes were on her work, but repairing engines came so naturally to her she had no problem multitasking.

Oh, where to begin. *Jacob is home. He kissed me. His grandmother thinks we're getting married. I want him so badly I can barely keep my hands off of him.* "Same ol' same ol'. You?"

"You remember that guy I met at that thing? He asked me out."

"Did you say yes?"

Mari shrugged. "I said maybe. He's cute, but who has time for dating? Between school, my part-time job and coming home on weekends, my calendar is full. Besides, there's nothing wrong with making him work for me if we do end up dating." Mari smiled. Grease and all she was a princess, the baby girl of the family, the charmer who could do no wrong. She shifted her attention away from the engine on the workbench and settled it squarely on Daisy. "Are you dating? Please say yes. You need a man, big sister. If you can't find one in Bell Grove then we'll get you to Atlanta and do some shopping for a suitable penis."

"Mari!"

"Well, one with a man attached to it. Believe it or not, you really can get them unattached. That's *not* what I had in mind. Just so you know."

Her sisters weren't blind to the sacrifices Daisy had made for them. They'd tried numerous times to fix her up with a friend, or a friend of a friend. A time or two Daisy had agreed, but it never worked out. Thanks to the current charade she finally realized that it never worked out with anyone else because she'd subconsciously compared every man she met to Jacob. Dammit, any man who gave her the time of day should come out well in that comparison.

Daisy's mouth went dry. She scooted her chair back a foot or so, tapped her foot against the plain concrete floor and finally worked up the nerve to say, "Jacob is back."

Mari dropped her wrench. The clatter of metal on concrete made Daisy jump. "What do you mean, *back?*"

"I mean, he's at the Tasker place for a couple of weeks. He's in for the big family reunion."

Mari's eyes hardened; she squinted. "That snake."

Yeah. Snake. Why couldn't she just agree with that statement and move on? Mari didn't need to know everything. She really didn't need to know anything. At the same time, Daisy was dying to talk to someone. "We've…kind of dated a couple of times since he's been back."

Mari clapped her hands on her cheeks in an expression of extreme frustration. "What's the difference between dated and *kind of* dated? Oh, Daisy, any man but him. He really is a snake. Mom would call him a scalawag. Dad would call him a lot worse. Jacob Tasker left you when you needed him most!"

"We left each other," Daisy said defensively, recognizing the words as painful but true. "Besides, it's not serious." She gave a dismissive wave of her hand. "It's just, kind of, sorta…"

"Spit it out," Mari said sharply.

Daisy did, telling everything. Well, almost everything. She wasn't about to tell her little sister that she still had the hots for her first love, that she was seriously considering sleeping with him just because she could, that when he'd put his hand on her leg she'd almost come apart.

She couldn't possibly admit to her sister that no matter how she tried to fight the feelings, she enjoyed seeing Jacob. She liked touching him, looking at him, hearing the timbre of his voice wash over her. Painful as it was, she liked pretending that they were still together. Was she a glutton for punishment or what?

The changing expressions on Mari's face, as Daisy filled her in on most of the details, told it all. Sadness, horror, frustration, indignation. All the emotions Daisy herself had suffered since Jacob had walked through her door.

But eventually the pretty face of the youngest of the Bells settled into a smug expression. Daisy knew that look, and she couldn't remember a time that anything good had come of it. Mari leaned back in her chair, forgetting her work for the moment. Her blue eyes sparkled and her lips quirked in a half smile. "Sunday lunch tomorrow afternoon, yes?"

"Unless I beg off." Daisy was considering doing just that. The thought of seeing Jacob again was both terrifying and exciting. She dreaded and anticipated the next date. "Since you're in town I really should just call and cancel…."

"Don't you dare." Mari smiled. "I'm going with you."

Jacob showered, washing off the sweat and dirt of an oddly satisfying stint of yard work. After that he spent most of Saturday afternoon in his room, working via computer and cell phone. The desk where he'd once done his homework now served as a place for his laptop. The chair was uncomfortable, but it would do, for now. Both were antique, as most of the furnishings in the house were. So were the bed, the bedside table and the lamp on that table. Everything in the room was older than he was, and a stark contrast to his modern apartment in San Francisco.

His job was one emergency after another, and had been since he'd signed on. That had never bothered him before this moment. In fact, he'd fed off the intensity. He'd learned to love being indispensable.

But now he realized that the job had stolen years of his life. He was home for the first time in a very long time, and he should be visiting with his parents, his little brother and his ailing grandmother. In a few days his older brothers were coming in. He hadn't seen them for years, and he didn't intend to spend the short time they were here sitting in his old bedroom, working.

What among the mountain of emails couldn't wait? What couldn't be handed over to someone else if it was critical? This was supposed to be a vacation, and he'd spent hours working from a distance when he should've been *on vacation*.

When he thought about abandoning work for a while, more than his family crossed his mind. Daisy. She had crawled under his skin, and the only way to take care of that would be to spend some time with her. Alone. Without the charade, without his family watching every move. He could forget that she wanted time and space, find an excuse to go to town, drop by her shop, and maybe walk her home. They could stop by the ice cream shop for a cone or a sundae. She used to be fond of strawberry sundaes…

Like she was going to go for that.

They were different people than they'd been seven years ago. They'd grown, matured, moved on. But he was discovering that neither of them had moved on entirely. A spark was still there. They weren't finished, not yet.

He wanted to get to know the new Daisy, the woman. He wanted her to get to know him. For that, he was going to need time, and dammit he didn't have much time left. Two weeks, and a large part of those weeks would be devoted to family. No choice there. But he'd make time for Daisy, he'd find a way. The odds were, they'd spend some time together and find out there was nothing left but that unexpected spark which was nothing more than an echo of the past. They'd have nothing in common, most likely. Normally Jacob knew exactly what he wanted and how to get it, but since coming home life had become more complicated. *The odds, most likely*…qualifiers that were not a normal part of his thinking process.

There was only one way to proceed. He was going to court Daisy and see what happened. Did he even remember how to do that?

Would she allow him to court her? When was the last time he'd even considered "courting" a woman? These days there was the hookup, the blind date, the one-night stand. Courting indicated something else entirely. Something more.

Another email came in, another minor emergency. Jacob read the email and then, he answered.

I'm on vacation. See you in two weeks and two days.

He pulled his cell phone out of his pocket and turned it off then he stored both the laptop and the cell on the top shelf of his closet, right above the acoustic guitar he'd left behind years ago. Would he have taken that guitar with him if he'd been any good? He'd always loved music, and really wanted to play, but he'd never gotten the hang of it. Had he given up too soon?

He slammed the closet door on the guitar, the cell phone and the computer.

It felt good. It felt really good.

He couldn't truthfully say that he had no second thoughts. There was the perfectly reasonable concept that if the company could do without him for two weeks they could do without him forever. He might not have a job to go back to. He didn't think that would be the case, but in the corporate world anything was possible.

In the end he decided he didn't care. Maybe he'd change his mind in a few days, maybe he'd panic over the possibility that his company would find out he wasn't indispensable. Maybe once he and Daisy were alone for an extended period of time, the echoes of the past would fade away and they'd be left with nothing.

At the moment what he wanted more than anything was to concentrate on Daisy without distractions. Hudson-Dahlgren paid him an excellent salary and incredible bonuses. He enjoyed his work.

But for the next two weeks, his project of choice was Daisy Bell.

Chapter Six

Daisy glanced in the rearview mirror. It wasn't that she thought Mari might get lost, no. She just felt a little surge of much-needed comfort as she was reminded with a glance that she wasn't alone.

She drove Jacob's rental car, and Mari followed in her own small pickup truck. Not only did Daisy have a way to get home without Jacob, once Sunday dinner was done, she felt as if she were going into battle with a staunch ally at her side. Until now she'd been on her own, one Bell against six Taskers. Those weren't good odds for any Bell. There were only two of them today; they were still horribly outnumbered, but Daisy felt empowered. Mari might be slight and deceptively cute, but she was also blessed with determination and loyalty. She wouldn't let her big sister down.

Their weapons of choice for this particular battle were Mississippi Mud Cake and Cajun Shrimp Pasta Salad. Mari was a great baker; Daisy had made the pasta salad, which was tasty but simple to prepare. When it came to cooking, Daisy was a big fan of simple. She'd put the pasta salad together early that morning and then stuck it in the fridge to chill.

They parked in front of the house, Daisy purposely choosing the parking space to the right, where there was a place for Mari to park directly beside her. She recognized Ben's car, which had been pulled in slightly crooked as if he always took up two spaces with his flashy little car. The others were likely out back, parked in the separate garage. Today would be another small family gathering of familiar faces. Only this time, Daisy wasn't alone. She had backup.

For Sunday dinner Daisy had opted for long pants and a lightweight long-sleeve shirt, leaving as little skin as possible exposed. She wasn't worried about what the Taskers thought about the way she dressed, wasn't trying to make up for Lily's scandalous little dress by covering up every inch of skin. She was just making sure there was nothing exposed for Jacob to touch.

Even if she wanted that touch, she knew it was a bad idea. No matter how out of control they were, her hormones would not rule her. She was master of her own desires. Captain of a long-neglected body. She was in charge of her own hoohoo. It was not in charge of her.

A thought that lasted until Jacob stepped onto the porch. No suit today, she noted. Jeans. A pullover shirt that clung to those muscles she wasn't quite used to. His hair was a little mussed.

This was the Jacob she remembered. Her heart lurched and thumped against her chest; for a moment she couldn't breathe. How dare he? Where was the blasted suit that reminded Daisy that Jacob wasn't hers anymore?

Mari, huge Mississippi Mud Cake in hand, walked briskly up the steps and placed herself directly in front of

Jacob. "Long time no see," she said, smiling sweetly. And then she kicked him in the shin.

He flinched, not because it was a particular violent attack, but because Mari had taken him by surprise. "What the hell was that for?"

"As if you don't know," Mari said softly. She was smiling when she continued. "Hurt my sister again and I'll gut you."

Jacob looked past Mari's shoulder and caught Daisy's eye as she came up the steps, the large bowl of pasta salad in her hands. "I think she means it."

"I do," Mari said. Five foot two and not much more than a hundred pounds, she was surprisingly fierce. Lily might be the sister people thought could take a biker in a bar fight if necessary—she was tall and dark-haired (by choice, if not by birth) and sharp-tongued and had a low threshold for bull, and there had been a short period of time when she'd worn nothing but black—but it was Mari they should've been afraid of. She might *look* harmless, but beneath the Barbie-doll exterior she was tough as nails.

Susan came to the door, and Mari scooted around Jacob to greet her and hand over the cake. Susan wasn't surprised to see Mari. Naturally Daisy had called to ask if it was all right if her visiting sister tagged along. The two women exchanged hellos and smiles. The screen door squealed and then snapped shut behind them, as they stepped into the house.

And there was no longer anyone between Daisy and Jacob. All that remained between them was a large bowl of pasta salad and her determination to remain in control. Daisy clung to both for dear life.

"Y'all didn't have to bring food," Jacob said. "We have more than enough."

Daisy didn't respond that he should've known they

wouldn't show up to Sunday dinner without bringing something. She stepped toward the house, toward him, steeling herself for the day ahead. "So, in spite of your insistence that the accent is gone, San Francisco hasn't cured you of your 'y'all.'"

Jacob smiled. "I wasn't home long before it came back." When she reached him he took the bowl from her hands. Their fingers brushed, and lightning shot through Daisy's body. She dipped her head, looked down at the boards beneath her feet so he couldn't read the emotions on her face.

The truth wasn't easy to accept. In fact, it was damn hard. Standing there with her heart in her throat, Daisy accepted the ugly truth. In spite of all her affirmations and determination, when it came to Jacob she wasn't in control of anything.

To Jacob's relief, there was no talk of weddings or wedding gowns over the dining room table. Maybe Grandma Eunice was distracted because Mari was there, and goodness knows this could not possibly be the same very young girl she remembered. Maybe Grandma Eunice was still sharp enough to realize that there was a reason Daisy hadn't been to the house for a couple of days, and she'd wisely decided not to push—for once. She likely wouldn't guess that Jacob had scared Daisy off with a hand up her very short dress, but she might assume there was trouble in the fictional paradise she'd created.

Strangely enough, it was Mari and Maddy who dominated the conversation. They didn't talk about the reunion or Tasker family business or the wedding. Instead they talked about people they both knew. Maddy was a couple of years older than Mari, but they had several acquaintances in common. And then they started talking about football. Yes, even in June college football was an acceptable topic of conversation at the dinner table. The others soon joined in the discussion, and everyone had an opinion. They talked about coaches and players and the fall schedule. Ben and Susan both made predictions about win-loss records. They were both *very* optimistic. It was nice; nothing was forced or false and there was lots of laughter around the table. Jacob was able to relax. After a while, so did Daisy. It was good to see her genuine smile, to watch her unwind, to hear her laugh.

When dinner was over, Jacob pushed his chair back and offered Daisy a hand. He wasn't sure she'd take it, but she did. Tentatively, and after a pause the space of a heartbeat, but she wasn't afraid to touch him.

"Walk with me?" he said, imagining a stroll around the property. Alone. He wanted to have Daisy to himself, even if it was just for a few minutes. The courting process had to begin somewhere....

"I can't." She slipped her hand from his, slowly, and then hid it behind her back as if he wouldn't dare to reach for her if he couldn't see that hand. "Mari is heading back to school this afternoon, and she needs to get packed and on the road."

"She can't pack without you?"

"I told her I'd help. Besides, she's my ride home."

"I'll be your ride." It was an offer touched with command. Not a question, but a very polite order.

"No, thank you." Her response was delivered in a calm voice, so sweet and unmistakably insistent.

He should've remembered that Daisy had always hated being told what to do. She could dig in her heels with the best of them. How the hell was he supposed to court her if she wouldn't spend even a few minutes alone with him?

Mari glared at him and mouthed, *Remember what I said.* Then, for effect, she drove an imaginary knife into her own stomach and stuck her tongue out in a brief, expressive demonstration of his upcoming, violent demise. The entire warning, if you could call it that, took less than five seconds, and if anyone else saw her they didn't let it show.

Of course, Grandma Eunice was the only one who needed to be fooled, and she was being wheeled out of the dining room. She always took an afternoon nap, and today she appeared to be fading fast.

"We really should go," Mari said as she rounded the table to collect her sister. "Remember, we need to call the critter man this afternoon."

"The critter man?" Jacob asked.

"Sammy Jenkins?" Mari said, as if he was an idiot for not knowing who the critter man was.

"I have squirrels in my attic," Daisy explained. "Mari and I both heard them last night, scurrying above our heads." She shuddered, a little. "Sammy doesn't work on Sundays, but he will take calls in the afternoon and set up appointments for next week."

"I didn't realize critter men were in such demand," Jacob said.

"You wake up to the sound of little paws dancing a jig overhead and you'll understand why," Daisy said.

Maybe this could be his way in. "There's no need to wait. I'd be happy to take care of your squirrels."

Mari laughed. So did Maddy.

"What's so funny?" Jacob snapped.

"Jacob Tasker, critter man trainee?" Mari said. "Yeah, like you'd get your hands dirty crawling into the attic."

How hard could it be? "I'd be happy to help, and I *do* work on Sundays."

"No, thanks," Daisy said, without her sister's venom or humor.

"But I could…"

Daisy glanced around the room and then lowered her voice. "Eunice isn't here, Jacob. We don't have to pretend for anyone else."

Those who remained in the room—Ben, Maddy and Mari—went still and quiet. Maybe they'd forgotten that this was all pretend. Maybe they could hear the pain in Daisy's voice the way he did. It was enough to put a man on his ass.

How could he convince her he was no longer certain he was pretending?

Not here, not now.

"Oh, your dishes," Maddy said. "Let's wash them up real quick…"

"I'll get them later," Daisy said. She backed away, obviously anxious to leave. No, not to leave, to escape.

To escape him.

"Gotta go!" Mari took Daisy's arm and they left the dining room together, their steps quick as if they really were escaping. And he supposed they were. It was Mari who glanced back, once, to stick out her tongue and flash a particular finger in his direction.

Jacob couldn't help but wonder exactly what time Mari would be headed back to school.

Finally they were gone! Eunice had pretended to be asleep, but her daughter-in-law had hung around for a few minutes, sitting in the chair by the bed, sighing now and then.

Perhaps she should feel guilty for putting the family through all this drama. Maybe one day, after Jacob and Daisy were married and had a child or two, she'd confess and they'd all have a good laugh.

Eunice rolled up and reached for her bedside phone. She dialed the number she'd memorized. A man answered.

"Is everything in place?" she asked, her voice lowered in case anyone was in the hallway outside her door.

"Yes, but Ms. Tasker, are you sure…"

"If I wasn't sure would I be calling you?" She put a command she'd worked years to master into her voice. If you looked up Steel Magnolia in the dictionary, you might find her picture there.

"No, ma'am, but…" The man wisely stopped speaking, and then he sighed into the phone. That sigh really carried over the phone lines.

"Do it," Eunice said sharply, "or I'll find someone else who will. I want everything to be put into motion this week. This needs to happen immediately." Anyone who had ever worked with or for her knew that if she wanted something, it happened. Maybe she didn't have a controlling interest in the business any longer, but she did control a large portion of the family fortune, and her reputation made it difficult for many old business acquaintances to refuse her requests.

She hung up the phone without a proper goodbye, leaving the man on the other end of the call sputtering a bit.

Eunice lay back down and relaxed. She smiled as she drifted toward sleep. By God, this was going to happen. One way or another…

Mari was gone, and the house was oddly quiet again. Even the squirrels in her attic were silent as dusk settled and the light in the house dimmed. Daisy had taken off her good clothes hours earlier, and had put on a pair of cutoff shorts and a blue tank top—an outfit more suitable for the late-June weather. She should be thinking about putting together a light supper, but she wasn't hungry. She'd eaten too much at dinnertime.

Then again, maybe her lack of appetite was Jacob's

fault. He had her turned inside out and upside down. As far as she was concerned, she could even blame him for the squirrels that had taken up residence in her attic. After all, she hadn't had any trouble with critters before Jacob had come back to town.

The knock on the door made her jump. Without looking through the glass, without asking "Who's there?" she knew who it was. It was as if when Jacob was near her body shifted into another gear.

If she opened the door and it was someone else, would she be relieved or disappointed? Did she *want* Jacob to be on her front porch? She did, even though she knew that letting him into her house was the worst thing she could do. Or the best. No, it would definitely be a bad idea!

She could refuse to answer, simply pretend she wasn't at home. She could yell at him to go away, and take the chance that she was right about who had rung her doorbell. If she prepared herself, she might even be able to sound as if she meant it.

She did neither of those things.

Daisy opened the door on a Jacob who reminded her too vividly of the boy she'd once loved. Tonight there was no suit, no preppy golf shirt. Even his posture had changed a bit, as if he'd finally remembered that he was home, and relaxed. He was still wound pretty tight, just not as tightly as he'd been the day he'd walked into her shop and asked for the favor that would turn her life upside down. He held a large woven sack in one hand, and a small paper bag in the other.

"Your dishes," he said, lifting the well-worn woven sack. He raised up the paper bag. "Strawberry sundaes."

Daisy hesitated a moment before she backed farther into the house, opening the door wide, silently asking Jacob to come inside. For a moment she actually convinced herself that they could share a strawberry sundae and then she'd send him on his way, but that delusion didn't last long.

It didn't last long at all.

Chapter Seven

Jacob hadn't been sure what kind of reception he'd get when he showed up at Daisy's door unannounced. Since his return to Bell Grove, she'd never been exactly happy to see him. But if he was going to court her, if he was going to try to reignite an old flame for the next two weeks, that would have to change.

So many emotions passed across her face when she opened the door to him, he wasn't certain he could register them all. Annoyance, anger, resignation, lust. Maybe the lust that seemed to flicker in her eyes was wishful thinking on his part. Maybe he used her as a mirror for his own emotions.

She invited him inside—a good sign, he thought—took the sack of dishes from his hand and set them down. After a moment's hesitation she took the sack of sundaes, too, and carefully placed it on the coffee table.

And then Daisy surprised him. She stepped into him,

wrapped her arms around his neck and pressed her body to his as she lifted her mouth to his and kissed him. There was no hesitation in the kiss, or in the way she melded to him. There was no uncertainty or anger in the mouth that devoured, in the tongue that danced. She was soft and certain, warm and gentle.

For a split second he was taken back to a time when he and Daisy had been together, when kisses like this one had been an everyday pleasure. But the flashback didn't last. That was then, this was now. And now was fine. Very fine. They were both different. Older, if not necessarily wiser. The past seven years had changed them both, had shaped the people they'd become. This wasn't an echo, it was something new. New and powerful.

Jacob's rational thoughts drifted away as he was swept up in the kiss, in the sensation of Daisy's hands on his neck and in his hair, in the feel of her soft, warm body against his, in the way her mouth and his connected. One small, soft hand slipped just beneath his shirt. Her fingers swayed there, matching the rhythm of her mouth. The kiss deepened; her breathing changed. He was lost, caught up in that place where nothing mattered but touching her.

If she stopped, she was going to kill him.

As that thought flitted through what was left of his brain, she did stop. She pulled her mouth from his—slowly, and with a reluctance he tasted—dropped her arms, and took one step away. It was all Jacob could do not to grab her and pull her back. He didn't. Instead he fisted his hands and took a deep breath. If this was her idea of torture, it was successful. He was definitely tortured.

And then Daisy surprised him again. She grabbed the hem of her tank top and pulled it over her head. After dropping the tank to the floor, she reached out and unsnapped his jeans.

"Daisy…"

"Don't talk," she said. "If you talk I might change my mind, and I don't want to change my mind."

He remained silent.

"Just this once," she said softly, not looking him in the eye. "I don't love you anymore, so don't go thinking this is anything more than it is, but we didn't end things between us properly. We never did really end us at all." She unzipped him, reached her hand inside his jeans, moved in close again. For a long, wonderful moment, he held his breath and allowed himself to just *feel*. "So we're going to get this out of our systems tonight. We're going to make love and say goodbye, and then we're both going to move on."

He would've agreed to chop off his right hand at the moment, if she'd just keep going, so he didn't argue.

"We were good in bed, Jacob," she whispered, her breath warm on his skin. "Maybe we screwed up everything else, maybe life screwed it up for us, but…we did this right."

He whipped off his shirt, as she had, and reached into his back pocket for his wallet. One condom wouldn't be enough, but it would have to do.

She wasn't wrong; they *had* done this right.

"You can speak, now," she said.

"Have I told you that you're more beautiful than ever?" he asked as he backed her toward the hallway.

"No." She smiled.

"It's true."

"You only say that because I'm mostly naked."

"Maybe."

"You're not looking so bad yourself," she said, walking backward very slowly, reaching up to brush her fingers against his upper arm, then his chest. "I'm glad you don't wax your chest. A little chest hair is a good thing on a grown man. You only had the one, when I last saw you without a shirt."

"You've been worrying about my chest hair?"

"Maybe just a little." She smiled, but then her expression changed, shifted slightly and he could see a concern there. Where had her mind taken her?

"No more talking," he said as they arrived at her bedroom door. She opened the door on the small bedroom, the same one she'd slept in as a child.

She sighed in relief as she backed toward the double bed. "Fine by me. Talking was never our strong suit."

For a moment, an unpleasant split second, Daisy had imagined what Jacob's life in San Francisco was really like. It wasn't a thought she'd wanted, wasn't one she'd reached for. But like it or not, she'd found herself wondering if he seduced other women with ice cream, if those other women seduced him with a kiss, if they touched his biceps and his chest—where thankfully a decent but not overwhelming dusting of chest hair grew—as he walked them to a bed to make love. She'd wondered if he looked at them this way, visibly on the edge of losing control, his dark eyes narrowing and going darker, his focus on her and her alone. When he looked at her like this she felt like she was the only woman in the world. Did he make other women feel the same way?

Then she let the unpleasant thought drift away. She forced it to disappear, she let it go. None of that mattered; nothing mattered but right now. One night, one last hurrah, and then she could truly let *him* go.

And she'd only lied to him once, when she'd told him that she didn't love him anymore.

By the side of the bed, illuminated by what was left of

the day's light streaming through the blinds, he finished undressing her, unfastening her bra and dropping it to the floor, pushing her shorts and panties down and off. He was anxious, but didn't rush. Ready, but not out of control. Naked, Daisy slipped her hands into his jeans again, this time shucking them—along with a pair of dark green good-heavens-was-that-silk boxers—down and off.

And there they stood with nothing between them but whatever lingering doubts might remain. Daisy had none. Did Jacob?

She was so ready, one touch and she'd be done. It had been so long, too long, and she already throbbed in places that she'd forgotten could respond this way. Jacob tossed his condom to the bedside table and laid her down on the bed. They kissed, easy and deep. It reminded her that until Jacob had come back to town she hadn't been kissed in a very long time. No one had ever kissed her like this, no one but Jacob. Was a kiss more intimate and important than sex? Was it the true moment of soul connection? It seemed that way, as their mouths came together and incredible sensations danced through her body.

She loved the feel of his skin against hers, loved the heat of his body enveloping her. Her body swayed up and into his, slid down as she attempted to bring them closer together. She was ready; she wanted him *now*.

But he was stubborn, moving just out of reach, making this moment last.

He gently spread her legs with his knee, lifted up and looked at her—his eyes holding hers for a long, powerful moment—and then he slid down and dipped his head between her thighs. Her heart thudded, and she grasped the sheet as he lightly flicked his tongue against her where she throbbed for him. One flick and then another, and then he moved away. It was maddening, and then he intensified his efforts and she crested hard and fast, with a jerk of her body and a cry of release and relief.

That done, he crept up over her body. "If I just have this one night with you, do you really think I'll make it fast?"

No, no, not fast, please. Slow. Easy. Stay a while. But she was breathless, unable to speak coherently. So she said nothing. She didn't need to say anything as Jacob kissed his way up her body. Slowly and well. She melted into the mattress, satisfied—for the moment—and languid. Happy to have Jacob with her, thrilled to have this fantasy come true. Maybe it wouldn't last, maybe it wasn't the way it had once been, but this was fine on its own.

More than fine. She felt alive, cherished, a part of something greater than herself. She felt like a woman.

Jacob had developed some serious and impressive control in the past seven years. For a split second she allowed herself to think about how and why he'd developed that control, but she let that go, as she'd let so many other thoughts go. Sex had always been fast and furious in the old days. This was different. Jacob took his time arousing her all over again, kissing, touching. Maybe his control wasn't perfect, though, maybe it wasn't as infallible as he'd like for her to believe. He was hard and ready and hot. When she touched him, when she attempted to wrap her fingers around him, he always gently but insistently moved her hand away.

The faint light that had been streaming through the window when they'd entered the room soon faded entirely. She could no longer see Jacob well. She couldn't see his face, or the way his hands looked against her skin. And still he played with her. No, not *with* her. He played her like she was his guitar and he was a talented musician, and she gave herself over to him.

And then he was inside her. Finally. Perfectly. Daisy

closed her eyes and let her body take over. They found a rhythm that was slow and easy, at first. It was nice, it was perfection. She had the brief thought that she could do this all night, happily giving herself over to the amazing connection of body to body, to the gentle movements that were so right.

All night? No. Her need and his grew, their rhythm changed, became more frantic, and she found herself gasping as he drove deep one last time and they both shattered. She clung to him, crying out softly, holding on for dear life as her body shook. *I love you* flitted through her brain and almost escaped, but she stopped the words from flowing out in the heat of the moment.

"You're amazing," Jacob whispered. "And to think, I came over here to volunteer to be your critter man."

"You would make a lousy critter man," she responded in a whisper, surprised she had the strength to speak at all.

Jacob raised up, propped his head in one hand and looked down at her. She could barely see his face, and she wanted to see that face while she could.

"Why's that?" he asked.

She smiled. "How do I count the ways? First of all, your suit would get dirty when you climbed into the attic. I suspect you have no squirrel traps or bait in your fancy rental car, and what on earth would you do if you came face-to-face with a squirrel or a raccoon or a possum? They don't negotiate."

"Do you think that's all I can do? Negotiate?"

"Analyze and negotiate. You've been doing it since you were twelve." She ran her hands down his side, reveling in the shape of him, his heat and flesh. "Of course, you do seem to have developed some skills you couldn't have dreamed of at twelve."

He leaned over her, and she could not miss the hope in

his voice as he asked, "Are you reconsidering your one night only stipulation?"

Daisy turned her face away, dipped her chin even though she knew he could see her no more clearly than she could see him. "No."

Get it out of our systems my ass. It was the middle of the night when Jacob woke. Daisy slept on beside him, out like a light. Naked. Rumpled and flushed and gorgeous. If he stayed in her bed he'd end up making love to her again, and without a condom. That was a chance they couldn't take. What kind of a jerk would he be if he came home, knocked her up and then left again?

So he grabbed his clothes and made his way out of her bedroom, being very quiet, though he didn't think Daisy would wake even if he slammed the door.

There was a night-light in the hall, giving off just enough light to illuminate the space so he didn't run into anything. Feeling like a thief, as if he were intruding, he crept down the hall to open the door on the master suite. It was just as it had been the last time he'd seen it. Same king-size bed, same blue and white striped bedspread. It had been seven years, and Daisy had changed nothing. This was her home, now, she lived here alone, and yet she hadn't moved into the master bedroom and made it her own.

If she hadn't done it yet she never would, and he was washed in a wave of sadness. What if she wasn't happy here, the way he'd thought? What if she was simply stuck?

He used the hallway bathroom, dressed and made his way to the living room. There on the coffee table, melted ice cream and pink strawberry topping leaked out of a white paper bag. Since there was no way he could sleep, Jacob cleaned up the mess, tossing the melted sundaes in the kitchen trash and wiping down the coffee table with a damp cloth. That done he placed the dishes he'd returned to her—his excuse for coming to her door—on the kitchen table. He had no idea where they should be stored, so that would have to do. All the while he tried to be quiet even though he was pretty sure nothing would wake Daisy.

As he puttered around the house, he thought about his decision to court Daisy. Courting was an old-fashioned term, but it was appropriate. And here he was, still smelling her, still feeling her. They hadn't had the first real date, and he hadn't brought her flowers or candy. The sundaes... well, they'd never gotten to the sundaes, so that didn't count. Where did they go from here?

Since she'd declared this was a onetime deal, maybe nothing had changed. He could still attempt to court her. Would she be receptive or would she kick him to the curb? Would she think the only reason he pursued her was that they'd slept together once and he was trying to get her into bed again? Not that he'd mind sleeping with her again, but he wanted more. He wanted everything. How could he convince her that a one-night stand wasn't enough?

That thought stopped him in his tracks. If a one-night stand wasn't enough, then a two-week affair wouldn't be enough, either. Not for him, hopefully not for her. If he still intended to court Daisy, to woo her, to win back her heart...what would happen after his time in Bell Grove was done?

When it came to business, he could analyze and plot and graph a problem into submission, but when it came to planning his personal life he felt woefully inadequate. And really, *what* personal life? Since he'd moved away from Bell Grove his life had consisted almost entirely of work and work-related events. It had taken seeing Daisy again to make him realize what he'd lost.

He'd be doing her a favor if he walked away and didn't look back. He wasn't here to mess up her neat, tidy life, hadn't intended to start something he couldn't finish.

Jacob collected his wallet and his keys and headed for the door. With his hand on the doorknob, he stopped. If he left, what would Daisy think when she woke alone? If he stayed, how could he *not* make love to her again? He stood in the dark, undecided. For a moment he noted the complete stillness. San Francisco was never still. All night long he heard traffic, sirens and people in the hallway outside his condo. In Bell Grove life didn't stop after dark, but it did grow still. He'd missed that stillness and hadn't even realized it.

He needed to go, to get out of here while he could. And yet his hand remained on the unturned doorknob. He made important decisions every day, but since he'd come home the decisions he'd been forced to make were different. This wasn't business, it was life. A life he'd ignored, a life he'd put on hold.

His grandmother, his parents, Daisy… Was this a temporary aberration or had his life just taken a sharp turn?

Chapter Eight

Daisy woke with the sun that cut through the miniblinds shining in her eyes. She blinked hard, rolled over to escape the annoying light, pulled the covers over her head and took a minute to remember what day it was.

Monday, her day off. She sighed, closed her eyes tight and settled into the mattress, still half-asleep and hoping to drift off again. Hadn't she been having lovely dreams?

Jacob hadn't been a dream. He'd been here. He'd been hers again, for a while. Since she had the bed to herself, she could only assume that he'd left in the night, while she'd been sleeping. Just as well. Given the situation, the morning after might be awkward.

Reality intruded and she couldn't go back to sleep. She didn't have to get up and go to work, but the critter man was coming to check out the attic. As if on cue, one of the cursed critters ran across the attic floor above her head.

Who cared about squirrels? She was still naked, a little sore and supremely satisfied to the marrow of her bones.

Jacob. She shouldn't give him another thought, but how could she not? Last night had been even better than she'd imagined it could be. Daisy opened her eyes slowly, threw back the covers and reached one curious arm out to sweep the other side of the bed. It was cold and empty. There wasn't even much of an impression on the pillow next to hers. He'd left a long time ago.

Well, what had she expected? She'd told him sex was a onetime deal, one last hurrah. Why would he stick around?

She rolled out of bed, checked out the clock and groaned. Sammy would be here in less than an hour, so she needed to shower and grab a bite to eat. Clothes would be nice. Daisy grabbed a robe from the closet on her way to the bathroom across the hall. She took a quick shower, pulled on the robe again and headed for the kitchen.

At the end of the hallway, she stopped. A right turn would take her to the kitchen, and that was the plan. But she glanced to the left, and there he was; Jacob, asleep on the couch. Dressed, his too-long body twisted to fit the too-short couch, sound asleep.

Daisy smiled. Relief washed through her, as real and tangible as the water that had washed across her skin moments earlier. Jacob hadn't left. He should have…she told herself she would have if they'd been at his place…but he was here. He'd stayed.

Why had she ever thought having sex with Jacob would make it easier to let him go?

Since he was sleeping, she allowed herself to just watch him for a few minutes. It wasn't like this was a chance she'd ever have again. Asleep he looked more like the man…boy…she remembered. In sleep he lost the facade he'd built around himself. That's what the suits were, she decided, a part of the facade that he'd built to keep others at a distance, to remind everyone, including himself, that he didn't belong here anymore.

But lately he'd been dressing more casually, relaxing, and last night there had been no distance—and no clothing—between them. None at all.

For a moment, a few seconds maybe, Daisy allowed herself to wonder what it would be like to throw everything away and leave Bell Grove to be with Jacob. She loved her home, her business, her friends, but had she mistaken serenity and a feeling of home for being stuck in a rut? Could she walk away from everything she had, could she leave her life behind? Not that he was going to ask her to do that, but if he did…

She no longer had her sisters to raise, that was true, but nothing else had changed. Her home was here; she belonged here. In California she'd be too far away from Lily and Mari, and dammit, even if they were grown they still needed her. And she needed them. She couldn't even imagine herself there, a small-town girl in a big city. And she couldn't imagine Jacob moving back here, leaving his job behind to work with his mother and Ben in the family business. If he'd been interested in that he would've done it years ago. No, Jacob would go back to work and she'd do…what? She doubted Bell's Beauty Shop and Small Engine Repair would successfully relocate to San Francisco. She found herself both excited and terrified by the very thought.

Not that Jacob would ask her…

Not that she'd go…

As she walked into the kitchen to start the coffee, she knew she should be sorry about last night.

But she wasn't.

She should kick herself for being weak, for giving in,

for taking what she'd wanted from—no, *with*—a man she still loved.

But she didn't kick herself. With a smile on her face she started preparing breakfast, wondering if Jacob was as ravenously hungry as she was.

Jacob woke to the smell of bacon and coffee. He was twisted into an unnatural position and his back hurt—damn couch—but he wasn't sorry he'd spent the night here. It would've been wrong to sleep with Daisy and then creep out of her house like a thief.

He rolled up, stood, stretched and walked to the kitchen. Daisy stood before the stove, turning bacon in an ancient iron skillet. She wore a short robe. He was pretty sure there was nothing beneath it. Her body clung to the satiny fabric. Did she know how sexy she was in that robe?

"Morning," he said, his voice gruff.

She didn't look up from her task, but she smiled. "Good morning. Are you hungry?"

"Starving."

"Me, too." She opened the oven door and peeked inside. "The biscuits are almost done. It'll just take a minute to scramble the eggs."

Jacob walked to the kitchen table. "I thought you didn't cook."

"This isn't cooking," Daisy argued. "It's breakfast."

He didn't argue with her, he just watched.

As she broke eggs into a bowl, she glanced over her shoulder and smiled. "The biscuits are frozen. Well, they *were* frozen before I put them in the oven. Full disclosure. I don't make homemade biscuits, so don't go thinking I've turned into Suzy Homemaker overnight. Eggs are easy. Anyone can scramble an egg."

"I want to spend the day with you." Jacob didn't want

to talk about biscuits and eggs. He had this suffocating sensation that time was much too short where Daisy was concerned. He didn't want to waste a single minute.

She shrugged her shoulders. "I suppose we can spend the day together, but be warned. I have an agenda. The critter man is coming by this morning, and then I have to go to the church and pick up some meals to deliver. That'll take at least two hours, more if anyone along the way needs their hair trimmed or styled. This afternoon I'm helping my friend Terry—do you remember Terry Hall? She's Terry Sanson, now, and she's got three kids!— anyway, I'm helping her paint her bedroom. Lavender. I don't approve of the color, but it's what she wants and it *is* her bedroom. Her husband doesn't care, so lavender it is. Then tonight..."

"Are you trying to scare me away?"

"No." She glanced his way. "This is my life...it's a perfectly ordinary start to the week. Monday the shop is closed, so I volunteer and help my friends and take care of problems around the house."

"And later tonight? After all that is done?"

Daisy turned and looked at him, squarely and strong. "I wasn't kidding when I said sex was a onetime deal for us. It was great, but don't think you'll be spending the night here on a regular basis, or well, *at all,* while you're in town."

Jacob kept a straight face as he said, "So, you're going to use me and then throw me away."

"Pretty much," Daisy responded in a bright voice, and then she turned her back to him to see to the eggs.

That robe was maddening. Short, clingy and beneath there were long legs and bare feet. Had he ever seen her in anything that didn't make her look sexy as hell? Daisy Bell would be tempting wearing a potato sack.

"What if I just want a date?" he asked, his eyes on the curve of her hip beneath the robe she wore.

Moving efficiently, ignoring his question for a moment, Daisy put breakfast on the table. Old china plates, silverware, cloth napkins. Coffee cups that matched the plates. Jam. Three kinds. She finally answered as she worked. "Why on earth would you want to go on a date? Men take women on dates with the hope that they'll *maybe* have a night like last night. We skipped the dating part and went straight to the real fun. I'd think you'd be grateful."

"Grateful?" He couldn't keep the edge out of his voice.

She frowned a bit, looked away from him for a moment. "Look, just eat. The critter man will be here in less than fifteen minutes, and I'm still not dressed. Oh, shoot, I didn't make grits. Do you want grits? All I have is instant, and they won't take…"

Jacob reached up and snagged Daisy's wrist. She went still and silent, but she didn't snatch her arm away, as she could have. "I don't want grits. I want you to sit down and eat with me." She sat, almost reluctantly, and grabbed a biscuit. Then she reached for the strawberry jam and butter, and set about fixing her biscuit as if all was right with the world and she had no other concerns beyond the butter to jam ratio. He glared at her. "And dammit, Daisy, I want that date."

Daisy took a bite of her biscuit, licked a dollop of jam from her lip and then she looked at him. She could glare, too. "No."

The critter man, Sammy, arrived right on time. If you had a snake, raccoon, fox, chipmunk or squirrel problem in the county, you called Sammy. He was in great demand, and the only reason he'd worked Daisy into his schedule today, so soon after her call, was that she cut his wife's hair.

Sammy was an odd man. Short and stocky, he had a face that was less than symmetrical and a complete lack of fashion sense. Today he wore baggy khaki pants, black socks and shoes, a Georgia Tech T-shirt, and his usual horn-rimmed glasses.

That made it a relatively good day for Sammy, fashion-wise.

"Come on in," Daisy said brightly, trying to ignore the fact that Jacob was standing right behind her as if he'd spent the night and they were a couple. That was half-right, she supposed. He *had* spent the night.

Sammy wiped his feet before stepping inside, his curious eyes landed on Jacob. He nodded. "Mr. Tasker. Good to see you."

They'd never met, at least they'd never been properly introduced, but it wasn't like everyone in town couldn't recognize a Tasker on sight.

"Call me Jacob." He stepped forward and offered his hand. Sammy wiped his hand on the side of his khakis before taking the offered hand and shaking briefly.

"Love what you've done with the place," Sammy said, turning back to Daisy and pushing his glasses up with his index finger. He leaned forward and glanced into the dining room. "The new window treatments are fabulous. Really fabulous."

Window treatments? She'd hung new curtains a couple of years back, but they weren't anything special. "Uh, thanks."

"This rug is new, isn't it?" He looked down, between his feet. "Beautiful, beautiful work."

"No. This rug has been here for twenty years." Maybe she needed to shop for a new one, but who had the time?

"The place looks great, really. Of course, it always did. I haven't been here in years."

Not since before her parents had died. How long before, Daisy had no idea. She didn't remember, but maybe her parents had had trouble with squirrels while she'd been in college and had been ignorant of the kinds of problems that came with caring for an old house.

"Do you want to check the attic?" she asked.

Sammy straightened his spine, looked around one last time and said, "Sure."

Daisy led the critter man into the hallway, grabbed the plain rope-pull at the end of the hall and with a yank released the attic stairs. For a moment she held her breath, half expecting the offending squirrel to run down the stairs and into the house. Wouldn't *that* be a disaster! But that didn't happen. Sammy turned on his flashlight, adjusted his belt and climbed up the creaking wooden stairs. As he neared the top he sniffed hard and often, and with his head stuck in the attic he said ominously. "I smell urine. Yep, yep, that's urine all right."

Great. She had squirrel urine in her attic.

"The next step is to determine what species of squirrel you have nesting here." With his body half in and half out of the attic, he shone the light of his huge flashlight around. "I don't see anyone here at the moment, but…ah, yes, that's how they're getting in, the little rascals."

Jacob asked, loudly enough for Sammy to hear. "What difference does it make what species of squirrel is nesting up there?"

Sammy took a step down, turned and poked his head out of the attic. The serious expression on his face was almost comical, and Daisy had to bite her tongue to keep from laughing.

"It's extremely important. What if the invaders are an

endangered species? What if the newest residents of this house are flying squirrels, or fox squirrels?"

Daisy tipped her head back. "First of all, I think *invaders* is more accurate than *residents*." They weren't exactly roommates. "And I'm sorry, Sammy, but I don't care if they're endangered or not." Daisy kept her voice calm but firm. She didn't want to annoy the only critter man for fifty miles. "I want them out of my attic."

"Flying squirrels and fox squirrels are not really endangered, not in these parts, but they're not exactly common tree squirrels, either." Sammy looked offended, perhaps on the squirrels' behalf. Daisy wondered how offended he'd be if he knew everyone—including his wife—called him the critter man behind his back.

"There are lots of places for small animals to hide up here," Sammy continued. "I'll set some traps, plug the entrances and we'll see what happens." He took another two steps up the ladder, moving more fully into the attic. He continued to sniff and ooh and ah. "Nuts!" he cried.

"Is something wrong?" Jacob asked.

"No, no, but I found a stash of nuts. Walnuts and pecans. Your little friends have been hoarding."

"They are not my little friends," Daisy said softly. Jacob looked at her. He smiled. Then he laughed, and a moment later Daisy was laughing, too. It felt good, not just to laugh but to laugh with someone, to share a joke. Daisy's laughter died quickly. She forced it to stop. The last thing she needed was to get any closer to Jacob Tasker than she already was.

Today should cure him of any misconceptions where she was concerned. If she was really lucky he'd be a jerk and that would make it even easier to cut him loose. She really, really needed to cut him loose, once and for all.

Sammy was in and out of the house for a while, up and

down the attic access ladder. He set traps and sniffed some more, and once again admired her window treatments. As he left he said he'd be back later in the day to repair the cracks that had allowed the varmints to slip into the attic in the first place. Those repairs he could handle from outside, so Daisy didn't need to be home.

When they were alone again, Daisy turned to Jacob. "Welcome back to Bell Grove."

"Is the rest of your day going to be as interesting as the morning?"

"Probably."

"Then I'm definitely in."

Daisy raised her eyebrows, crossed her arms defensively. Maybe this wasn't such a good idea, after all. "You know how word spreads in a small town. If you spend the day with me, by sundown word will be out that we're back together. Even though we're *not*."

"I can handle that. You?"

No, not really. "Of course."

Jacob moved closer, he lifted his hand as if to cup her cheek, or pull her in for a kiss. For a split second Daisy considered letting him continue. After all, last night had been wonderful, and she could still feel him, smell him. And here he was, willing and able and wonderful. But she pulled away sharply and ducked beneath his arm, making a cowardly escape.

Jacob had forgotten where he'd come from, and he'd apparently forgotten why they didn't work together for more than one wonderful night. A day driving around the most rural parts of the county should cure him of that forgetfulness. Those she delivered meals to were needy, but they weren't always easy to get along with.

"Don't get any ideas, Tasker. Spend the day with me or not, it's not a date and we're not sleeping together again."

"Whatever you say."

She could hear in his voice that he hadn't given up. Too bad, because she meant what she'd said. Jacob Tasker could break her heart all over again, but only if she allowed him inside it.

Chapter Nine

Eunice Tasker sat at the table in her bedroom where she usually took her lunch, munching on chicken salad and green grapes and drinking sweet tea. For dessert she'd have chocolate cake, because she was by golly old enough to eat whatever she pleased without worrying about calories or fat count or sugar. According to Lurlene they were almost out of chocolate-covered cherries, and that would not do. That wouldn't do at all. Eunice had three chocolate-covered cherries every night before bed, served to her on one of her good china plates, with a linen napkin in case any of the juice dribbled. Since she was an expert at eating chocolate-covered cherries, it had been a long time since she'd had need of that napkin. Susan complained that it wasn't easy to find her mother-in-law's favorite treat after the Christmas season had passed, but she managed.

Eunice was not going to sacrifice her chocolate-covered cherries.

The truth of the matter was, at better than eighty she was healthy as a horse. Her legs weren't as strong as they had once been, and her hips and knees gave her trouble every day—and would until the day she died—which is why she relied on the wheelchair. If it hurt to walk, why should she walk?

Doc Porter had told her she'd live to be one hundred or more, and she planned to prove him right. Not that she could share that tidbit of information with her family. Not right away.

Eunice looked out the window and smiled. Jacob hadn't come home last night. He'd left here with Daisy's freshly washed dishes, and he hadn't come home. Finally! Maybe Daisy wasn't as stubborn as she'd first thought.

For a few minutes, just a few, she considered calling her friend in Atlanta and changing her plans, but in the end she decided against making that call. One night of love might not be enough to push Daisy into Jacob's arms. She might still need a little extra incentive. Everything was playing out very nicely. Why take a chance by changing her strategy now?

Not for the first time, Eunice felt a little guilty. Just a little. She could see that her family was suffering, thanks to her game. She knew they were on edge, waiting for her to go completely bonkers or fall over dead. But the guilt didn't last long. She already had a plan to cover her tracks. After Jacob and Daisy were married, but before the family brought in the new physician Eunice had promised to see after the reunion, Doc Porter would discover that his patient didn't have dementia after all, that her confusion was the side effect of a blood-pressure medication. He'd change her medication, for appearance's sake, and Eunice would miraculously improve. Voilà.

Though she had to admit, playing at being bonkers had been a lot of fun. And Caleb really could use a wife…

Jacob had forgotten how different everyday life was in Bell Grove. In San Francisco he didn't know his neighbors. His life consisted of work, a couple early mornings a week at the gym and the occasional work-related social event.

In Bell Grove everybody knew everybody. Work was necessary, but so was church, and the occasional town social, and helping your neighbors when they needed it.

Daisy thought nothing of spending her only weekday off driving all across the county delivering meals. And it wasn't like she dropped the prepackaged meals off and ran. She visited, laughed and expertly repaired more than one head of disheveled hair. She cleaned one man's kitchen in record time, and removed a splinter from a woman's trembling hand. At one house, she fed three dogs and a cat.

He didn't miss the joy on the faces of those Daisy visited as she walked in the door. They genuinely liked her, and why wouldn't they?

She was gorgeous, she had a killer body and she had a laugh that Jacob felt to his bones. But it was her heart that set her apart, her heart that made her unlike any other woman he'd ever met. Every chore she took on, she accomplished with a smile.

Jacob found himself a topic of conversation among those Daisy visited. He was a curiosity, at the very least. So far they'd dropped off meals to two elderly ladies, one ancient gentleman and a middle-aged woman with a broken leg. He was familiar with them all, the names if not the faces, though he couldn't say he knew even one of them well. They knew who he was, but other than a name and the memory of a child or a young man who'd once lived in Bell Grove he might as well have been a complete stranger.

They knew *his people,* and that was enough to serve as an instant introduction. You'd think he was a long lost relative, the way some of them acted.

None of the older folks were very subtle. They winked and waggled their eyebrows, and the old man looked at Daisy then glared at Jacob and announced that it was "about damn time." Daisy insisted on telling them all that she and Jacob were just old friends, but none of them bought it.

He didn't buy it himself.

Their last stop was the most isolated on her route. The small house had to be close to a hundred years old, but it had been well maintained. From the bumpy dirt road that approached the house from the south, he could see a window air conditioner at the front of the house. Given the size of the place that one unit was probably enough to cool the entire house. The wide front porch was so overgrown, all that was visible from their angle, as Jacob parked in what might've been a designated parking space, were a few weathered steps.

Daisy jumped out, opened the rear passenger side door and retrieved the last meal and a bag containing a bottle of water, a soda and a carton of milk. She didn't seem at all concerned about entering the house, even though it looked like the setting for a horror story.

And that was *before* an elderly, stick-thin woman with an Einstein-ish hairdo burst into view, brandishing a shotgun. She held the weapon as if she knew exactly how to use it.

Instinctively Jacob jumped in front of Daisy. He threw out an arm to push her back and she stumbled. He heard her bounce against the car, mutter "ow" and "what the hell?" The woman on the steps lowered her shotgun.

"Sorry," she said in a gravelly voice. "I didn't recognize the car."

"Not a problem," Daisy said. She stepped around Jacob, glared at him and then looked at the armed woman and—strangely—she smiled. "This is my friend, Jacob."

The woman adjusted her grip on the shotgun as if she were thinking of lifting it up again. "Jacob *Tasker?*"

"Yes," Daisy said crisply.

"I shoulda known. He has the look of his grandfather at that age." She finished that observation with a spit to the side, as if she were ejecting the bitter taste of his name out of her mouth.

This crazy woman he didn't remember at all. Maybe when he heard her name…

Daisy moved toward the house with her offerings. Jacob stayed close behind her. "Yes, I suppose he does look like his grandfather. But now, that's not his fault, is it? It's not his fault that he's a Tasker, either. There's not a thing he can do about the name he was born with." Standing on the bottom step, now, too damn close to the shotgun, Daisy turned to him. "Jacob, this is Vivian Reynolds." She looked up again. "Miss Vivian, be nice to Jacob and I'll braid your hair."

The old woman sighed as if being nice to a Tasker was going to be a great sacrifice, but she did finally nod and head across the porch and into the house. Jacob sighed himself when they stepped into the house and the Reynolds woman set her shotgun aside, leaning it into a corner near the front door. "Can't be too careful when you live out in the boonies on your own."

Jacob glanced around the living room, which was clean and nicely furnished, though none of the furnishings were new. There were knickknacks, but not too many. An older television with a single recliner in front of it. A small book-case filled with paperback books.

A smallish dog came running from the back of the house. A bundle of hairy energy, the brown dog danced and sniffed around one visitor and then the other, then finally returned to the feet of his mistress. They were a matched, scruffy pair, both of them in serious need of more care than a little time with Daisy would provide.

"Why do you stay out here all alone?" Jacob asked. "Wouldn't you be better off living in town?"

The shotgun-toting woman turned an evil eye on him. "Well, ain't you the nosy one?"

"Sorry. But you did mention being careful because you live out in the boonies on your own."

She huffed, and when she moved her head her wild white hair danced. "If I could afford to move, sonny, I would've done it years ago. This house is paid for, the land is mine. It's all my sorry excuse for a husband left me when he passed, near twenty years ago."

"I'm sorry to hear that."

"Sorry that he's dead, or sorry that he didn't leave me a pot to piss in?"

Jacob wondered if it was too late to head outside and wait in the car. Ninety-plus degrees and sunny, it was still not a bad idea. Nothing he said was right. "Both, I sup-pose."

Daisy directed Mrs. Reynolds to the chair in front of the television, which was dark, and slipped out of the room. Jacob was tempted to follow her, or else excuse himself and wait outside in the heat.

Vivian pierced him with a glare. "So, Eunice is your grandmother."

"Yes, she is. Do you know her?" Jacob racked his brain,

but he had no memory of the Reynolds' family. He couldn't recall ever hearing the name Vivian Reynolds.

"I do. Is she still a conniving, backstabbing bitch?"

"Miss Vivian!" Daisy said, as she returned to the room with a brush in one hand and a handful of bobby pins in the other. "What a thing to say."

"I'm old enough to speak the truth when it suits me," she argued, settling back in her chair as she awaited the brush. She closed her eyes and looked almost content as Daisy began to brush out the tangles. It wasn't an easy job.

"Have you been using that conditioner I gave you?" Daisy asked.

"Now and then."

"Every time you wash your hair, use it," Daisy instructed firmly.

"All right, all right, if you insist." Vivian puckered her lips. "Like anyone cares what I look like. Hell, like anyone's going to see." She looked down at her dog. "Buster doesn't care if my hair is tangled or not."

Jacob glanced around the room. The only pictures displayed were two snapshots of a young Vivian and a handsome man who had a rough look about him. No pictures of children or grandchildren. No smiling photos of family and friends. Did she have no family or had she chased them all away?

"*I* see," Daisy said, "and so do the volunteers who come by on Wednesday and Friday. You know I would be happy to take you to the grocery store instead of bringing your groceries in, and when you need to see Doc Porter there are always people in the waiting room. If you'd start coming back to church you'd see all kinds of people."

"Last time I was at church that dirty old man George Hayes made a pass at me."

Daisy laughed. "He asked you out for ice cream and offered you a ride home."

"Like he didn't expect something in return," Vivian muttered under her breath.

Jacob wouldn't allow himself to smile. With his luck the old woman would pick *that* precise moment to open her eyes.

"I do hope you're not sleeping with this...this *Tasker*." Vivian didn't wait for a response. "First of all, you deserve better than a Tasker. And secondly, no man is going to buy the cow when he can get the milk for free."

Daisy sounded calm as she replied, but he couldn't miss the new tension on her face. "Jacob is just here for a visit. He lives in San Francisco."

"Hell, if I was a Tasker I'd move as far away as I could, too," Vivian said. She opened her eyes and glared at Jacob. "You had the good sense to run away from that sorry family of yours. Why did you come back?"

"My grandmother is very ill."

Vivian made a huffing noise and closed her eyes. She squirmed a bit and finally she said, "Good." But there was something strangely *complicated* in her voice. She wanted to be glad that Eunice Tasker wasn't well, but she wasn't. Not entirely.

Daisy quickly transformed Vivian's hair, taking her from Einstein to simply disheveled. For a few minutes, while Daisy worked, everyone was silent. Even the dog. Then Vivian spoke, and her voice was different. Reluctantly softer. "What's wrong with her?"

Jacob explained, about the wheelchair. About the dementia. He didn't tell her about the ruse he and Daisy were participating in. He'd prefer to keep that in the family, if he could.

When he was finished, the old woman said, "Eunice

and I used to be best friends, a lifetime ago. We grew up together." Her words were clipped, precise. "I thought of her as if she were a sister, until she stole my boyfriend out from under me." Her eyes hardened. "That would be your grandfather, sonny."

Well, that explained a lot. "I'm sorry. I didn't know…"

"Of course you didn't know," Vivian snapped. "I did marry, a few years after Eunice and Charles, and I loved my husband deeply. But we didn't have much, and we never had children of our own. Do you know how much it hurt to see Eunice…" The woman took a deep breath and exhaled slowly. "But that was a long time ago. I don't suppose I should blame you." And yet her voice made it clear that she *did* blame him…

In Jacob's mind, Grandma Eunice had always been an old woman. He couldn't imagine her as a young girl with a best friend. Maybe laughing and dancing, whispering about boys…stealing her best friend's guy. That part wasn't all that hard to believe. For as long as he could remember, his grandmother had found a way to get what she wanted.

"Tell me about her. And you," Jacob added. "Tell me about those days."

It took a while to comb all the tangles out of Miss Vivian's fine, white hair. It always did. As she brushed, Daisy listened. She didn't know a person alive who didn't like to talk about themself and times gone by. Jacob had smoothed things over considerably by asking the old woman to talk about herself and her friend.

And apparently they had been very good friends, once upon a time. Miss Vivian talked about sleepovers and dances, skipping school and fishing. She talked about the time before they'd had a falling-out over a boy, and before she was finished the older woman was smiling in a way Daisy had never seen.

She finished with a story about two sixteen-year-old girls and a litter of puppies.

Daisy finished the braid and secured it. Next week she'd have to do it all again. Without Jacob. He'd disappointed her by not turning his nose up at those she visited, by pitching in when he got the opportunity. He'd taken an infirm woman's garbage cans to the street and had swept a kitchen or two. He hadn't uttered a word of complaint or judgment.

But best of all, he'd asked Miss Vivian to talk about herself. And then he'd listened. Miss Vivian always looked and obviously felt so much better after Daisy's visits, it made her wonder if she wouldn't be a completely different person if she wasn't so isolated.

Daisy settled her hands on Miss Vivian's bony shoulders. "I have an idea. Why don't you come to dinner with us one night at the Tasker House?"

The answer was immediate and held no room for negotiation. "I'd rather starve than eat in that woman's house. I'd rather have ground glass for supper than eat at Eunice's table. I'd rather eat cat food out of the can than give her the satisfaction."

Jacob didn't look as if he thought it was a very good idea, either, but he said nothing.

Daisy didn't give up. "Don't be that way. I'll give you a ride. I can do your hair, maybe even your makeup, before we go to the house. Don't think of it as having supper with 'that woman,'" she added. "Think of it as visiting with an old friend who might not be here six months from now."

Instead of another immediate refusal, Miss Vivian pursed her lips.

Jacob said, "Think of it as an opportunity to talk about

the old days one last time. Fishing and dances, puppies and cutting class. It's been a very long time, and…"

"Fine, fine," Miss Vivian said. "If you two are going to twist my arm I guess I have no choice but to agree."

Behind the older woman's back, Daisy smiled.

"How about Friday?" Miss Vivian said. "Friday is a lousy TV night. I won't miss anything if we make it Friday. There's a baseball game, but I should be home in plenty of time to see the last few innings." She scoffed. "It's not like I'm going to hang around after dinner is over."

"Friday it is," Daisy said, heading toward the bedroom with the brush and what was left of the bobby pins.

Behind her, she heard Jacob add, "Leave the shotgun behind."

Chapter Ten

Jacob pulled his car to the curb and shut off the engine. Daisy turned to him, smiled, then leaned over to give him a quick, easy, perfectly natural kiss. He was right there, and she just couldn't help herself. It had been a good day; he'd been a good sport. He'd not only stayed with her as she delivered the meals to those who needed them, he'd helped her help Terry paint her bedroom a hideous shade of lavender. With the three of them working it hadn't taken long. Of course, Terry had started before they'd arrived, so there hadn't been all that much to do.

Wanting Jacob was one thing. Realizing that she still loved him...she could live with that. *Liking* him was another matter entirely. It was a complication she could do without.

Daisy pulled away. Slowly.

"Are you going to ask me in?" Jacob leaned toward her, mirroring her movement away.

Daisy shook her head. "No." She couldn't ask him in. If she did they'd end up in bed again, and she was determined to remain in control of this situation.

He didn't press her. Maybe because he understood her reason.

"When do I get my date?" he asked.

Daisy laughed. "You don't! I think I've made it clear…"

"I threw myself in front of a weapon for you today. Don't you think that should earn me a little consideration?"

"It was just birdshot," Daisy argued.

"Just birdshot," he repeated.

"Not that Miss Vivian would've shot you." She shrugged. "Maybe," she added in a lowered voice. "She's not particularly fond of Taskers."

"One date or I'll camp on your front porch."

"That would be so uncomfortable for you. Maybe I can spare a pillow to make your stay more comfortable." She tried to sound nonchalant, when in fact the idea of Jacob right outside her door was torture.

He didn't give up. Had he ever? "One date or I'll hire a mariachi band to stand in your front yard and play until you change your mind."

"You know I hate mariachi music!"

"One date or…"

"Fine," she conceded. "Though I'll have you know it's only the threat of mariachi music that made me change my mind. One date. Nothing fancy. Maybe this weekend…"

"Tomorrow."

There was a note of finality in his voice, and she was forced to remember that Jacob was a master of negotiation. He was determined to succeed in anything and everything, and always had been. He didn't always succeed—his poor guitar-playing skills proved that—but he didn't give up.

She wondered if he still played the guitar or if he'd abandoned the pastime entirely, the way he'd abandoned her.

Daisy knew when she was fighting a losing battle, and to be honest she wanted that date with Jacob. This time they would end it finally and completely before he left for California. This time she wouldn't be left hanging and hoping and waiting.

It was going to end, *they* were going to end, but there was no reason she couldn't enjoy the little bit of time he was here.

He took her face in his hands. "I'll walk you to the door."

Daisy sighed. "You'd better not."

"I'm not ready to let you go just yet."

And she wasn't ready to let him go, which was all the more reason to make him stay in the car. Daisy shook her head as she turned away from Jacob and opened her door.

"So," she said as she exited the car, "when are you going to tell Miss Eunice about the guest you're bringing to dinner on Friday?"

"I think it should be a surprise, don't you?"

"We'll have to tell Miss Vivian about the fake wedding business," Daisy said, leaning down to look into the car. "Otherwise she'll be very confused."

"We'll fill her in on the way. I have a feeling she won't feel at all bad about putting one over on my grandmother."

"Probably not."

She pulled away, reluctantly, and Jacob called out, "I have the connections to round up a mariachi band and have them here in less than an hour. Don't forget that!"

Daisy laughed. She felt amazingly lighthearted and happy as she all but danced to the front porch. Jacob watched her go; she could feel his eyes on her. He didn't even start the engine until she unlocked and opened the front door.

Once inside the house, she leaned back against the closed door and shut her eyes. Listening to him drive away, she sighed. This was supposed to be helping; it was supposed to be a way of finally and completely letting go.

It wasn't working. And tomorrow night she actually had a date with the man she was still in love with.

A man who would never choose her over his career. Who would never put her first in his life. After all these years of caring for others, she needed to feel like the most important thing to someone.

The house was so quiet…so lonely. Even the squirrels had gone silent, or else had departed completely, leaving Daisy entirely on her own. She could feel and hear her own heartbeat, could hear the ticking of the clock over the mantel. It had never seemed so loud before, as if it were counting off the seconds of her life.

Or counting down the seconds of the little bit of time Jacob would be close by.

It took every ounce of determination Daisy possessed not to run outside and chase Jacob down the street. She'd smiled as she'd left him sitting in the car, but as she stood alone in the only home she'd ever known, a few annoying tears slipped down her cheeks.

"I called the house and told Lurlene that I wouldn't be home."

"Yes, she passed the word on. But she didn't say where you were, and I was worried sick!"

Jacob felt like a fifteen-year-old who'd been caught sneaking out. He was thirty-one, an adult who shouldn't have to explain to his mother where he'd spent the night. All things considered, it shouldn't be much of a mystery.

Lurlene wheeled Grandma Eunice into the foyer. It was likely not a coincidence that she appeared when she did. She'd heard his car, and come out to say hello. Jacob looked at his grandmother and, for the first time, saw her as a young girl. He tried not to picture the kind of young woman who would steal a good friend's boyfriend, but instead attempted to see the girl who'd fished and skipped school and babied puppies.

"Where's Daisy?" Eunice asked, looking past Jacob to the front door.

"She won't be here tonight. It was a long day and she wanted to get to bed early."

Eunice smiled, briefly. "Well, perhaps tomorrow. She still hasn't tried on her wedding dress!"

Jacob shook his head. "Sorry, it won't be tomorrow."

"Why not?"

"Tomorrow night we have a date." He winked at Eunice, who seemed very pleased by his announcement.

"Well, then, you two have a good time. Another day this week, then."

Jacob thought about Friday, and wondered if he should tell Grandma Eunice that an old friend would be joining them for dinner. He hesitated. He was already rethinking his impulsive invitation. If Grandma Eunice reacted to Miss Vivian the way Miss Vivian had reacted to her, then the night could turn ugly.

But he didn't think that would be the case. They'd been good friends, once, and now they were both alone. Alone in different ways, but still, surely an old friend would be welcomed. He said, "Tonight after dinner, why don't you get out some old photos and tell me about Grandpa."

She smiled. Like Vivian, talking about the old days was not a chore. And though her memory of recent events was fuzzy, at times, she remembered those old days as if they'd been just yesterday.

"Of course. It's such a shame that your Grandpa Charles passed before you were old enough to remember him."

"Yes, it is."

"He was very handsome in his day, you know. You look very much like him."

So he had been told.

Grandma Eunice seemed to be in a very good mood, bright and with it...until Ben and Maddy arrived, and she mistook her youngest grandson's wife for the new maid.

They didn't have a new maid.

The Tuesday workday passed quickly, customers coming and going while Daisy's mind was on the coming evening. It was a minor miracle that she didn't butcher a single head of hair while she was thinking of the night ahead. What should she wear? Where would Jacob take her? How would the evening end?

She knew how the evening *should* end. She'd leave him sitting in his car while she ran for the safety of her house. Alone. Again. After making it very clear that they were through. But oh, he made it so difficult to do what she *should* do!

Eventually she would have to end it. Truly end it this time, not just drift apart. She needed to look Jacob in the eye and tell him that they were done, that it had been nice while it lasted, that a part of her would always love him but they didn't have a chance of making it work so why put themselves through the misery of trying?

Daisy didn't want to think about that reality tonight. She wanted to let go of her worries and enjoy the evening for what it was. Old friends who made great lovers enjoying one another's company. Jacob would leave, and it would end, but maybe she should enjoy his company while he was close by, and hers to enjoy.

On her way home—it such a pretty day she was walking again, in spite of the heat—Daisy pulled her cell phone from her purse and dialed the Tasker House. Jim Tasker answered, and he fetched his son without asking a single question or trying to engage in polite conversation.

"What should I wear?" Daisy asked after Jacob said hello.

"Do you have a little black dress?" She loved the timbre of his voice. Even over the phone it was sexy and powerful, and oh, she was in much too deep when the sound of his voice made her squirm.

"I do, not that there's any place in Bell Grove to wear it."

"I made reservations at a Brazilian restaurant in Atlanta. Wear the little black dress. I'll pick you up in two hours."

She didn't get to Atlanta often. A couple times a year to shop, maybe, and she had been to a few concerts and ball games in the past few years. But for the most part she lived her life right here in Bell Grove. She'd never had a date take her all the way to Atlanta to eat.

Okay, black dress. But which shoes?

The critter man's truck was parked in front of her house. Shoot! She wanted to have the entire two hours to get ready. What was she going to do with her hair? Which bra? There were three possibilities when it came to shoes. Did she want to go for wowza or comfort or something in between?

There were also three bra possibilities. Also wowza, comfortable or something in between. Decisions, decisions.

A neighbor who had a key to the house had let Sammy in, and he'd collected the squirrel traps from her attic. They had served their purpose. He promised to release the squirrel-invaders on the other side of the county. It was unlikely, he said, that they would find their way back to this part of town and if they did, well, he'd already taken care of the access to her attic.

He was disappointed that the varmints were common tree squirrels.

Daisy started to suggest that squirrel stew might be an option, but then she saw the cute critters in their cages. Even if they were rats with bushy tails and good PR, and even if she would never have kind and fuzzy feelings for the critters the way Sammy did, they were, well, not stew worthy. Catch and release was fine by her.

Sammy didn't stay long, thank goodness. She wrote him a check, asked about his family, and when he asked she told him where she'd bought her curtains. Okay, so maybe he was a little odd, but he *had* gotten the critters out of her attic. He even seemed to genuinely like the rodents.

Not every man could be like Jacob. Handsome, sexy, driven…and not content to live in a small town where everyone knew everyone else and the pace of life was slow and easy.

That thought put a damper on her mood as she got ready, but by the time she was done she was feeling bright again. She wouldn't have Jacob for long, so she might as well enjoy him while she could.

The wowza shoes won.

As did the wowza bra. Just in case.

She was gorgeous. She took his breath away.

"Tonight I like the suit," Daisy said as she stepped onto the porch. "It's dashing, and appropriate."

"I don't look like the tax man showing up at your door to harass you?"

She shook her head, and her long, soft, pale hair swayed. "Not at all."

What he wanted to do was take her back inside and make love to her again. Surely she had something to eat in her kitchen, even if she didn't cook any more often than she had to. He'd be happy with a bowl of cereal.

She locked the door, and he took her arm. He walked her down the sidewalk to the driveway, where he'd parked behind her car instead of on the street, as he'd been doing since returning to Bell Grove.

Jacob placed himself between Daisy and the car door, which he had every intention of opening for her.

But not yet. He placed a hand at the base of her spine, pulled her close and kissed her. Not a searing kiss, not a prelude to sex, but a tattoo. A brand. *You're mine,* the kiss said. *Deny it all you want, but you're mine.*

With his hand still on the small of her back, he felt her tremble. Her lips opened to him, she leaned in closer. He released her, because if he didn't they'd never make it into the car.

Daisy blinked fast a couple of times, and when he opened the passenger door for her she slid into her seat carefully, as if her legs were unsteady. She didn't say a word until he took his seat and started the engine.

"Do you think anyone saw that kiss?" she asked.

"I don't know, and I don't care," Jacob said as he backed into the street and pointed the car toward Atlanta.

"That's because you don't live here. I do." She looked at him; he kept his eyes on the road but he could see her out of the corner of one eye. Damned if he didn't also feel her eyes on him. "I thought I heard a car go by, but I'm not sure."

If the kiss affected her the way it did him, what she'd heard might've been the roar of an engine…or the rush of her blood and her heartbeat, spinning out of control. "I don't recall," he said calmly. "And let's be honest. My car was parked in front of your house all night a couple of days ago. The nosy neighbors are probably already talking."

She sighed. "I know. But if anyone saw that kiss there will be no doubt about what's going on."

Going on. As in continuing? "Do you care?"

She sighed, fiddled with the small black purse in her lap. "No, not really. I'm a grown-up. I suppose it's perfectly natural for me to have a man stay over on occasion."

I suppose. Which meant it was unusual for her to have overnight guests. He couldn't express how relieved he was to hear that. Not that he could tell her as much. "Your decision that it was a onetime deal…"

"Still stands," she said quickly. And then she sighed. "I suppose. Though you will be gone soon, and it's not like either of us is involved, and…dammit, Jacob, why did you kiss me like that?"

Dinner had been great, well worth the drive into Atlanta. Jacob's company had been even better. He'd talked about his job and all the traveling he'd done; she told him about running the shop and what was going on with her sisters. Jacob had been her friend before he'd been her lover, and even though she didn't want to, she still liked him. You could love someone and not like them much, and you could certainly like someone without loving them. Jacob was the complete package, for her. A friend. A lover.

And in a couple of weeks he'd be back in California, and she'd still be here. Alone. She'd thought if she could finish things with him she'd be able to move on, meet another man…build a life.

But she was finding herself falling in deeper and deeper,

more in love than ever. She couldn't even imagine building a life with another man. And wasn't that a shame?

Having Jacob in her life, however temporarily, was like having a gallon of death-by-chocolate ice cream in the freezer, knowing it was the last gallon of death-by-chocolate ice cream she'd ever have. Maybe one day she'd settle for vanilla, when she really wanted ice cream and that was the only flavor available, but when? Not until she no longer craved death-by-chocolate. Not until she could no longer remember how it tasted, how it felt on her tongue. And what if she settled for vanilla and it turned out to be butter pecan inside a vanilla carton? She hated butter pecan.

Why should she limit herself to one bowl of death-by-chocolate ice cream? Why should she have one bowl and then dump the rest? What a waste. Shouldn't she finish up the entire gallon before it was gone for good?

It was late when Jacob walked her to the porch. A few lights were on in the neighborhood, but no cars—or people—were on the street. He parked in the driveway behind her car again. The streetlamp lit their way to the porch, where her front porch light cast a yellowish light over them. At the door she opened her purse, removed the house key...and then turned to Jacob and lifted her face for a kiss. He obliged, and this kiss was as deep and moving as the one that had started the evening. But it was also more. It was a beginning.

She pulled her mouth from his, grabbed his tie and hung on. "You make me break every promise to myself," she whispered. "I promise myself that I won't like you, I promise myself that I won't care, I tell myself that one night with you will be enough, that it's all I need. And then... and then you ruin it all. Worse than that, you make me indecisive. I'm not indecisive, Jacob, I don't make an important decision and then change my mind because of a kiss."

"Are you inviting me in?" Jacob rested his forehead against hers.

"I am."

"If I come inside I won't leave until morning."

"You better not," she said. "And I do hope you're more prepared than you were last time."

"I'm ever the optimist, so yes."

Daisy spun around, unlocked the door and pulled Jacob inside by the tie. "You and your suits," she said as she closed and locked the door behind him, leaning against it and looking him up and down. "Take it off."

Daisy had crawled out of bed to put a CD in her portable player. The music was something new, a soft sound with a slow, relaxing beat. When she tried to crawl back between the covers Jacob intercepted her, took her hand, and drew her away from the bed and more closely into his embrace. They danced away from the bed and across her bedroom floor. Naked.

He wasn't a great dancer, and neither was she. They didn't have a lot of space to maneuver in the small bedroom. But they could move together—man, could they move together—skin to skin, swaying to the music in the half light that cut in from the bathroom across the hall. That light fell across her shoulder as he spun her around, it lit her face, and he wondered how the hell he'd survived the past seven years without her.

Maybe it was the feel of her skin against his, the memory of her beneath him, the lingering sounds of her laugh and her sigh and that catch deep in her throat, but Jacob had the sudden and unwanted revelation that a part of him had been missing all this time. He'd lost himself in work, and along the way he'd allowed himself to forget what it was like to be more. To have someone to talk to at the end of the day. To have a person in his life that he couldn't live without.

He didn't want her for two weeks, wouldn't be satisfied with a fling. He didn't want to court her, enjoy her company for a too-short period of time and then go back to the way things were. No, he wanted all of her, heart, body and soul.

"Come back to San Francisco with me," he said, the words pouring from his mouth without thought.

"Really?" She backed away sharply; her eyes caught his and held them.

"Really."

Daisy moved in again, resting her head against his chest. She drifted closer, and her hands skimmed his back. "Maybe you should think it over and ask me when we're not naked."

"Why?"

"Because you're not thinking with the big head, at the moment." It was meant to be a tease, he could tell, but there was also a touch of uncertainty in the words. He'd hurt her. He didn't want to hurt her ever again.

"I won't change my mind."

Her hands settled on his hips. They continued to dance, skin to skin, barely moving, caught up in the movement and in each other. "Don't you travel a lot?"

"Yes, but what…"

"What am I going to do while you're gone?" He heard the anxiety in her voice. "If I were to go with you, if you still want me in the morning and you ask again and I say yes, if…" Her breath caught on one of her many ifs. "I don't know anyone there. I don't even know anyone on that side of the country."

"You know me," Jacob argued. "You could travel with me part of the time, and you'll meet other people there. You'll make friends right away. Who wouldn't love you?"

She hesitated, but not for long. "I have friends here, a business…a home that's paid for. My sisters are close by. I can't just put my life on hold and move because the sex is great."

Did she think that was all they had? Was she right? "We can work it out." He'd said that seven years ago, but nothing had worked out. Did she remember that, as he did? His invitation had been foolish, not well thought out at all. He was never impulsive, but that's what asking her to come home with him had been. Impulsive, his heart speaking instead of his head.

"You don't need me, Jacob," she whispered. "This is just…old memories, the past, one last hurrah…"

"What if it's not?" He pulled her closer, dipped his head to whisper against her ear. He didn't have all the answers. He only knew he wasn't ready to let her go. Not yet. "I need to think about it," she said. "And so do you."

Daisy let her hands drop to his butt cheeks and squeeze gently.

"Are you trying to change the subject?" he asked.

"Desperately."

Maybe she was right. He wasn't thinking things through; he hadn't allowed himself to work out the details. He worked long hours; he traveled around the world. As much as he liked the idea of coming home to Daisy every night…she'd be miserable. He didn't want to make her miserable; he wanted to make her happy. So simple. Not so easy. He should've thought this through before asking her to come home with him, should've anticipated all her questions and had answers ready. Instead he'd just blurted out the invitation without a single thought beyond keeping her.

He didn't want his brain to get caught up in all the problems, not right now.

"I didn't realize how much I'd missed you until I walked into Bell's Beauty Shop and Small Engine Repair and saw you standing there," he confessed.

"I've missed you, too," she said, but there was a sadness in her voice that told Jacob she wasn't even considering leaving Bell Grove behind to be with him. She'd missed him; she'd miss him again, when he was gone.

The dance, her flesh on his, the maddening knowledge that they didn't have forever…his brain was spinning, and he didn't like it. Life was black and white, good and bad, right and wrong. When he was with Daisy, everything was washed in shades of gray.

Jacob lifted Daisy off her feet and carried her back to bed. He tossed her onto the mattress; she bounced and laughed and then he was on her, his mouth against hers, his fingers on and in her body. There was no question about *this,* no shades of gray when they were in bed together. And then he was completely inside her and nothing else mattered.

Who wouldn't love you? Jacob had asked as they danced, skin to skin, in her bedroom.

What Daisy had wanted to say was *You. Or am I wrong about that? Do you love me? Say the words, make me change my mind. Tell me I'm more important than any career. Tell me that you love me.* Instead she'd offered a logical argument.

For as long as she could remember, logic had been a large part of every decision she made. What choice had she had? Thrust into the role of guardian too soon, taking on a demanding job at a young age and with no warning, she'd done what she had to do. Logic told her that she and

Jacob didn't have anything in common anymore. Logic reminded her that no matter how wonderful it was having him back in her life for a while, it couldn't last. There was much more than the countless miles between them. They lived in different worlds.

She loved having Jacob in her bed, waking up, reaching out, touching his body. How would she ever go back to sleeping alone? It felt so right to have him beside her, as if he should've been there all along, as if he'd never leave her again. Tonight—this morning—he didn't creep out of bed and move to the couch. No, he stayed with her all night. They made love, they talked, they laughed. They danced.

As the sun came up, Jacob slept on. Daisy couldn't. Thoughts of what might've been, what might still be, kept her awake. Maybe she should've just said yes when Jacob had asked her to go to California with him. Maybe she just should've trusted her heart and her body and dismissed all the logical reasons why she shouldn't go anywhere with him. It wasn't like Bell Grove was going anywhere. If she went to California and it didn't work out, she could always come home.

With her tail between her legs and defeat in her broken heart. That was what held her back, the very real possibility that her heart would be broken all over again. But was that very real possibility any worse than not taking a chance?

Jacob was still sound asleep when she cuddled up against him, put her mouth next to his ear, placed a hand against his hip and whispered, "Yes."

Jacob wasn't sure what had awakened him, but slowly and surely he came awake. It was still dark out, but the clock told him morning was coming. Daisy was nestled against him. Her breathing and the way she held her body told him she was not sleeping.

He rolled into her, wrapped his arms around her and held her close. "You should get some sleep."

"I can't," she said, her soft words warm against his skin.

"Am I keeping you awake?"

"Yes."

Had he been snoring? Taking up too much space in the bed? "I can move to another room, sleep on the couch if I'm…"

Her hold on him tightened, and she threw one leg over his as if to hold him in place. "Don't you dare go anywhere. Not tonight," she added in a lowered voice.

It was so natural to tilt her face up and kiss her. She was right there, in his arms, so close she was almost a part of him already. The kiss deepened, her hands wandered and so did his.

She's mine. I'll never let her go again.

Yet as much as he wanted to believe that, he knew that nothing had changed. The clear light of day dispelled some of the emotion from the previous night. Her life was here and his was not. She *wasn't* his anymore and might never be again; and when he left Bell Grove it was very possible he'd have no choice but to let her go.

Chapter Eleven

"What? Is this some kind of a joke?" Daisy felt the floor beneath her spinning. Why now? Everything had been going so well. She'd hummed like a complete loon as she'd walked to work today, leaving Jacob asleep in her bed. Naked and rumpled. Beautiful. She'd smiled as she'd waved to neighbors who were walking their dogs or sitting on front porches drinking coffee. Her body ached, but it was a good ache. The song she kept humming was one they'd danced to last night.

She'd wondered more than once if Jacob would ask her to go to San Francisco with him when they weren't both naked. She wondered if she'd say yes while he was awake and could hear her.

Logic was highly overrated when it came to love.

It had been such a wonderful morning…for a while. Her short-lived happiness had come crashing down around her without warning, as if the universe was displeased that she was content. As if it wasn't in the cards for her to have everything she wanted.

Daisy—and her parents before her—had rented this space from the Chestnut family for more years than she could count. They hadn't had an actual lease since before her folks had died. The rental agreement went month to month, and they discussed expenses if they went up or down. Of course, expenses never went down. Still, she'd never felt the need for a lease. In this part of the world a handshake was as good as a contract, anyway.

Well, apparently that was no longer the case. Martin Chestnut was standing in front of her, his face a little pale as he explained what had happened. Someone had bought up this entire side of the square. Every space, every store. Including hers. The offer that had come his way had been too good to pass up.

She had a week to get out. A week! The other tenants along the strip would be allowed to stay; they'd simply be paying a new landlord. But the new owner wanted *this* space emptied.

There was a lifetime of memories here, she made her living here! The house was paid for, but she did have living expenses. Mari was still in college. Daisy needed food, she had to pay her property taxes and that old house was in constant need of some sort of repair. She had savings, but not enough. Maybe she had been considering leaving town with Jacob, if he asked again. But facing the reality of leaving everything behind was very different from fantasy.

"I'm sorry," Martin said, not for the first time. "But I'd be a fool to let a chance like this one pass me by."

"Yeah, yeah, you said that already." She waved off his offered excuses. "Who's the buyer? What do they plan to do with the space? Do you know of another space I could move to, at least temporarily?"

Even as she asked, she knew another space wouldn't do. It was in *this* space that her parents had lived and laughed, *here* that she still felt their presence, some days.

All idyllic thoughts of a new life elsewhere had been ejected from her head. Another chance with Jacob wasn't a done deal anyway, it was just a dream. A lovely fantasy fueled by sex and memories. Belle Grove was home; this shop was *hers*. Well, apparently not as much hers as she'd thought.

"I don't know, I don't know, and no. Sorry." Martin backed toward the door as if he expected her to shoot him in the back if he dared to show it to her. "I'm thinking of retiring soon, and this was just…"

"Too good to pass up," Daisy snapped. "Yeah, I got that."

When he was gone, Daisy collapsed into her client chair, breathless. She felt as if someone had pulled a rug out from under her. Her business! Everything she'd worked for! Her home, her way of life, all of it just *gone*. For a while she allowed herself to panic, to imagine the worst—which included homelessness and complete destitution—and then her heart slowed and a strange clarity washed over her.

It wasn't hers, not really. This shop, her home, they were all she had left of her parents. This was *their* life, *their* dream. Had she been trying to keep them alive by stepping into the life they'd left behind? Was that what held her here?

Even though it was legally hers, this shop had never been her dream. She'd taken over because it had seemed the best choice at the time. The only choice, to be honest. She'd had sisters to raise and the insurance money had only gone so far. It wasn't like her folks had expected to die too soon and made plans accordingly. Daisy loved her home, but she still slept in her old bedroom because she couldn't make herself move into the master suite that had been her parents'. That was their home, still, not hers.

She had stepped in and taken over their life, and somewhere along the way she'd given up on building one of her own. Why had she never seen that so clearly before this moment when the business was being yanked out from under her?

Recognizing what she'd been doing made it possible for her to truly think beyond today for the first time in years. She'd loved her parents dearly, loved them still, but she couldn't bring them back. She couldn't replace them, either. Tears filled her eyes, dribbled down her cheeks, and she mourned her mother and father all over again. It still seemed wrong to walk away from everything they'd built, to let it die as they had died, but maybe it was time.

If Jacob asked her again to move, if he made the offer when they both weren't naked and thinking with something other than their brains, she'd definitely say yes. No second thoughts this time. Even if he didn't ask, even if that opportunity had passed…it was time for her to move on, time to start something new.

New.

Her initial panic faded away entirely. Yes, she'd miss her friends if she left Bell Grove, and she'd certainly miss her childhood home. But that's all it was, her *childhood* home. Her life had just opened up in an unexpected and oddly exciting way, and once she pushed past her initial panic she realized that she'd just been set free.

She had a little savings, and if she could sell the house quickly she and her sisters would have a sizable bit of cash to split. That would help with Mari's college expenses. She could sell the furniture, too. Looking at it objectively, there was very little in her home that she'd want to take with her. A few keepsakes, but other than that it could all go.

She was *free*. Daisy found herself smiling and crying at the same time, planning ahead as she mourned the past. Soon enough the tears stopped. The smile remained.

Daisy spent the afternoon calling her clients. She squeezed as many as she could into the next few days, but left a couple of days clear for cleaning out the shop. She called Lily and Mari, and explained to them what had happened. They were initially horrified on her behalf, but she was no longer horrified for herself and once she explained that to them, they were reluctantly happy for her. She heard the hesitation in their voices and wondered if they, too, hadn't felt as if something of their parents remained as long as Daisy kept the shop and house as they'd always been.

She didn't tell them that Jacob might be a part of her new life. That was still up in the air, a variable. She was hopeful that variable would work out the way she wanted it to, but until then she'd keep it close. If he broke her heart again she'd keep it to herself. There would be no need to burden her sisters with her pain—which would also mean sharing her foolishness with them. No, for now she'd keep Jacob and those possibilities to herself.

She called the house, but Jacob didn't pick up. Why would he? It wasn't his house. He had a cell phone, but she didn't have the number. Come to think of it, in the past few days she hadn't seen that phone at all. She'd tell him the news later, and maybe he'd take the opportunity to ask her again to leave with him when he left town. She had to admit, the timing would be perfect.

Daisy was putting her house up for sale.

She was closing her business.

It was scary, but there was also a strange sense of excitement inside her. She didn't know where she'd go, she wasn't even sure what she wanted to do, but one way or another the last of the Bells was about to leave Bell Grove for good.

Jacob drove out to Tasker House not because he wanted to leave Daisy's place but because he needed a razor and a change of clothes. Daisy had shared her shower, soap and shampoo, and she'd found him an unused toothbrush with the name of her dentist stamped on the side, but he needed more. If nothing else, the razors in her bathroom were unacceptable.

Before he'd left the house yesterday he'd made sure his mother had known not to expect him home. He hadn't added "If I'm lucky," though to be honest he hadn't been positive Daisy would ask him to stay.

Not until he'd kissed her.

Tonight he'd ask her again to come to San Francisco with him. While they were both fully dressed and she couldn't accuse him of asking only because he was carried away, caught up in the moment. It might take time to convince her. She had the house, her sisters…business concerns. He would have to make changes himself. He couldn't work the kind of hours he and his company had come to expect, couldn't devote himself entirely to work if he had a woman in his life. But he was suddenly certain they could make it happen. He *wanted* to make it happen.

He found his mother sitting on the front porch swing, drinking tea, looking as sour as the lemon slice in her beverage.

"Good morning," he said.

"Good afternoon." Susan's response was sharper than was necessary.

Jacob, wearing the suit he'd worn last night but without the now-rumpled tie, headed in his mother's direction. "What's wrong?"

There were new lines on his mother's face, a strain no amount of makeup could hide. "What isn't wrong? Your grandmother is more of a trial every day. In the past couple of years she's run off every caretaker we've hired to help, and will only tolerate me or Lurlene and we both have our hands full without taking care of her. Thank goodness Ben has taken on so many of the business responsibilities, but to be honest I miss it. I want to get back to work." She smiled a little. "Your little brother is more than competent but I enjoy working, and I like being needed for my brain. You know very well that the Cyrus Tasker branch of the family doesn't have the good sense of a fence post, and the Clyde Tasker branch has sold almost everything away. Uncle Carlton is the only one with any sense, and when he dies, well, I don't even want to think about it. He's pushing ninety, you know. Your father would rather play golf and drink beer with his friends, but he does help out at work when I need him. He's no help with your grandmother, though, because she still sees him as a child." Her smile was gone, and her eyes shone bright. She didn't let a single tear fall, though. "And Daisy. Really, Jacob, how could you take up with her again, after everything she put you through?"

Jacob leaned against the house and looked down at his mother. "Everything she put *me* through?"

"Yes! She broke your heart...don't think I didn't see that. She should've...she could've..." Her lips pursed and the line between her eyebrows deepened. "Oh, who am I kidding? Daisy didn't do anything wrong, and neither did you. It's all my fault."

Jacob was accustomed to his mother's dramatics, but this one surprised him. "Your fault?"

The dam broke and tears ran down Susan's face. This was a woman who never cried, no matter how bad things got.

"I didn't want you to be saddled with a ready-made family, not at twenty-four. I pushed you to move on, to leave Daisy behind. I did my best to make sure her sisters were not a responsibility you'd have to bear." She balled her fists. "I even...I even made sure she knew how happy you were in San Francisco, how well you were doing there. It's easier to blame her, to twist my memories of that time around and forget my part in it all, but...I did everything but tell her outright that you didn't need her."

His heart constricted. "Whatever happened between me and Daisy is on us, not you."

"You say that, but I could've helped. I could've made things easier for both of you, and I didn't. I sat back and watched Daisy give up everything. She did a wonderful job of raising those girls." She wrung her hands—another unusual gesture. "So I quit going to town to get my hair done. I started shopping in places where I knew I wouldn't run into her. I avoided Daisy, because every time I looked at her I felt guilty."

"We can all look back and see what we should've done," Jacob said calmly.

"I was so wrapped up in the business, in seeing that you boys got a good start to your adult lives, I convinced myself that I didn't have time to take on another responsibility. I loved the idea of being more businesswoman than mom, of not having a houseful to take care of, and I didn't want to take on raising two young girls. I was selfish, Jacob. Horribly selfish. Now Daisy is here, day after day, playing this ridiculous game with you and the guilt is worse because I see how much you two care for one another. If

I'd offered to take the girls in, if I'd pushed the two of you together instead of doing my best to tear you apart…"

"I don't think Daisy would've agreed to leave her sisters here, not even with you," Jacob said.

"But…but I could've done something to help. I should've done something. Anything."

Jacob sat beside his mother and put an arm around her shoulder. For a moment they just sat there. She sniffled, but her tears didn't last.

"The blame is mine, not yours," Jacob said calmly. "If it makes you feel any better, I never believed what you said about taking on Daisy and her sisters being too hard, I never took that argument to heart. That's not the reason it didn't work. I got caught up in a new life, and I suppose the same thing happened to Daisy. We were young, and we let what we had fall apart all on our own."

"I can hardly look at her without regretting all I did. And even more, I feel horribly guilty about what I didn't do. I didn't help…all I did was make matters worse. She'll never forgive me."

"You're going to have to get past this, Mom," Jacob said. "Because if I have my way you'll be seeing a lot of Daisy."

She looked up at him.

"I'm going to pack a bag and stay at her place for a few days, if she'll have me," Jacob said calmly. "And if I'm very lucky, she'll agree to move to San Francisco with me." If he left here without her, no matter how good his intentions were, he feared they'd grow apart all over again.

"The mother of my grandchildren will hate me," his mother said softly.

Grandchildren? "She doesn't hate you."

"She doesn't like me much, either. Not that I've given her reason."

"Daisy hasn't agreed to anything yet," Jacob said with

a tight smile. "And you're getting ahead of yourself talking about grandchildren." Way ahead. He was thinking of living together and seeing how things went, getting to know one another again, having Daisy in his bed at the end of every day.

"I'm not ahead of myself, you're horribly behind. No one can watch the two of you together and not realize that you're in love."

First *grandchildren,* then *love.* The words shouldn't come as a surprise to him, shouldn't hit him with an almost physical force, but they did. He liked Daisy, he wanted her, she was like no other woman. Was that love?

His mother sniffled, lifted her head and looked him in the eye. "Don't ask her to move in with you."

Not again! "Mom, I…"

"Marry her, Jacob. She deserves nothing less."

Daisy was about to head for home when Martin Chestnut came back into the shop. He looked every bit as serious, and nervous, as he had that morning. She'd have to let him know that she was no longer upset, that it was okay…

"I got to thinking, after I left," he began.

"It's all right," Daisy said.

"No, no, it's not all right at all. At first I was just excited about the money, because the offer was so good. I was thinking about paying off the mortgage on the house, and retiring earlier than I'd thought I could. But after you asked who'd made that generous offer I got to pondering. I called my lawyer and asked him to do a little digging. He made a few calls, he asked all the right questions, I guess." Martin fidgeted, he was sweating, and though it was a hot day it wasn't that hot. And she had the air cranked up high.

"What did you find out?" Daisy asked, suddenly curious.

"The offer was routed through a couple of lawyers, like, you know, there was something to hide."

Daisy's spine went rigid. She tingled from head to toe, not in a good way but with an instinctive fear. She knew what was coming; she heard it in his voice. *No. Please, no.*

"It's a Tasker," Martin said. "Someone with the last name Tasker is trying to buy the downtown buildings."

Chapter Twelve

Daisy walked home slowly. She didn't hum, as she had that morning. She didn't wave at neighbors as she passed by. Her body and her brain were both numb. She hoped with everything she had that Jacob wasn't still at her house.

She wanted to kill him. Even before he'd asked her to go to California with him, he'd set a plan into motion to make sure she had no choice in the matter. The offer had seemed so spontaneous, as if he'd been as carried away by the moment as she'd been, but that wasn't the case. As usual, Jacob Tasker had come up with a plan to get what he wanted. Her.

A part of her wanted to believe that he hadn't had anything to do with what was happening, but nothing else made any sense. She'd tried to come up with another reason, an alternative, but there was no other logical explanation. He was playing her, had been playing her since the moment he'd walked into her shop. And it *hurt*. It hurt more than she'd imagined was possible.

Why was she surprised? It was Jacob's MO to do whatever was necessary to get what he wanted. He didn't lose. Ever.

He'd rip her livelihood out from under her to make sure she had no options other than him. Did he really think she was so weak? Did he think he could frighten her into packing up and following him to the other side of the country? Well, he was wrong. She *wasn't* weak and she had options. She had plenty of options that didn't include his sorry ass!

Again, Daisy suffered a moment's doubt. It was true that Martin hadn't specifically said *Jacob* Tasker was behind the sale, but who else could it be? What other Tasker would go to the trouble? It didn't make any sense to buy the property for one of their businesses. Downtown Bell Grove was much too small and insignificant to be of use to the company. The fact that hers was the only space that had to be vacated immediately was definitely suspicious. She tried to think of anyone else besides Jacob who might be behind the purchase. Ben probably didn't have the money. He and Maddy were big spenders, and she couldn't imagine that his savings were impressive. Not yet. Caleb and Luke had cut their ties to Bell Grove long ago. Jim? No. If it had been a golf course…maybe. Susan didn't even like the idea of Jacob and Daisy together. She wouldn't lift a finger to push Daisy out of town, and perhaps into her son's arms, and given the timing Daisy couldn't think of any other reason for the unexpected sale.

It couldn't possibly be coincidence that a Tasker was driving her out of business. Yeah, there were a lot of Taskers around, but she'd ruled out everyone else in Jacob's family—but him—she didn't think any of the cousins were even aware of her existence. Downtown Bell Grove functioned, but it wasn't great investment property by any stretch of the imagination.

That left Jacob. He wanted her, he'd set his sights on her the way he did a floundering company he thought his employer could take over and fix. Or destroy. Would he try to fix her and then, when he discovered that he couldn't, dismantle her? Maybe he'd get bored with her, once she was entirely his and there was no more challenge. Maybe once he had her, he wouldn't want her anymore. Like a fool she'd fallen in love all over again, and he'd just been playing a game. A game he fully intended to win.

Jacob Tasker always won.

She couldn't believe she'd let him get under her skin this way, that she'd fallen in love with him, that she'd actually allowed herself to *like* him. Well, at least one part of her original plan was still in place. There would be no growing apart, this time. No nagging feeling of romantic matters left unfinished.

They were finished, all right. This time she would tell Jacob to his face that they were through.

Jacob packed a bag this time, before driving to Daisy's place. There was just a little more than a week until the reunion. They'd be moving back and forth between her home and Tasker House for the next few days, but he wasn't going to pretend anymore that he wasn't with her. One hundred percent, he was with her.

Maybe tonight she'd agree to move to San Francisco with him. His mother's mention of marriage had nagged at him all afternoon. She said that was what Daisy deserved, and she was right. But he wanted to wait. It was too soon; this had happened too fast. They didn't know each other as well as they should before he took that big step. He'd get her to San Francisco, see how they worked there, make sure what he was feeling wasn't entirely physical. He didn't think that was the case, but still, he tried to be more cautious these days than he'd been at twenty-four. He liked to take his time and think important decisions through.

If he'd done that seven years ago, he would never have left Daisy behind. But that was then, this was now. Life was more complicated than it had once been.

Jacob pulled into the driveway and parked behind Daisy's car, blocking her in. The car had been there when he'd left, so she'd obviously walked to work. Was she home? He had to assume she was, by this time of day. If she wasn't home he'd wait on the front porch, sitting in the rocking chair there, waving at neighbors who passed by. He grabbed his bag from the backseat, locked the car and all but danced to the front steps. Maybe tonight she'd give him a key, so when he locked the door behind him as he left he'd be able to get back inside.

Daisy met him at the door, and when Jacob saw her face he stopped in the middle of the big porch, several steps from the doorway. He no longer felt like dancing.

Her cheeks were flushed red, her lips thin...she was furious.

"What's wrong?"

She pushed the screen door back and stepped onto the front porch, poised as if headed into battle. "As if you don't know."

He didn't know what was coming, but it couldn't possibly be good. "I really don't have any idea..."

"I'll make it easy for you." She stopped two steps away from him. "I'm not leaving Bell Grove. I *will* find another place for my business, and I *will* survive without you. I have never needed a knight on a white horse to come riding into town to rescue me, and if I did, well, we both know you'd be lousy at the job. I could've used a little rescuing seven years ago, but that girl is long gone. These days I take care of myself."

Jacob dropped his bag onto the porch. "Daisy, tell me what happened." He tried to remain calm, because one of them needed to be and she was anything but.

She waved an agitated hand in his direction. "Martin Chestnut came into the shop today and told me I have a week to get out. A *week!* Someone with the last name Tasker bought the building, and I'm being evicted. Like I need to tell you that. No more games, Jacob. No more games!"

"You don't have a lease?" He was horrified, and that horror came through in his voice.

Her face turned a deeper shade of red. "That's all you have to say? No, I don't have a lease," Daisy snapped. "I haven't needed a lease until now. How was I supposed to know you'd buy the building and kick me out to make sure I can't stay here?"

The situation was looking increasingly ugly, and to be honest the comment about him being a lousy white knight still stung. Even if it was true. Before he could do anything, he needed to know more about what had happened between the time she'd left the bed and this moment where she looked at him with panic and fury in her eyes and in the set of her jaw.

"I have no idea what you're talking about. What makes you think I'd do something like that?"

She was angry; he was insulted.

"Who else?" Her voice was too high-pitched, too sharp. "I've tried to come up with another explanation, I really have, but nothing else makes sense. You've always been one to get what you want, one way or another. You asked me to leave here with you, I didn't immediately fall on my knees in gratitude and say yes, and the next thing I know..."

Now *he* was angry, and he remembered some of the arguments they'd had when they'd been together. Daisy could dig in her heels. So could he. "Do you really think I have the connections to put together a sale between two in the morning when I asked you to move to San Francisco with me and whenever you got the news?"

"I figured you were planning ahead, covering all your bases." Finally he saw a flicker of doubt on her face. The mouth softened, and she looked down at the floorboards of her porch. Her eyes narrowed, and her body seemed to unwind. "It wasn't you?"

"No." The word was clipped, and held no room for debate.

"You swear?"

Jacob's hands clenched into fists; he felt a tightening in his chest, as his temper rose. "Daisy, if I was going to do something so underhanded, would I use my *name?*"

Daisy shuffled her feet. Her cheeks flushed. She'd been angry, and apparently she hadn't thought through the details. She'd lost her temper, and now she looked to be regretting it. A little bit, at least. "Well, apparently the buyer tried to cover their tracks, but they didn't do a very good job of it. All Martin could find out was that the buyer was a Tasker, and I can only think of one Tasker who would..."

"Me." So much for remaining calm. The last of his taut control washed away. "Someone is attempting to run you out of town, and you assume it has to be me."

"Who else, Jacob? Who else would *care?*"

He took one step closer to her. "I don't know. It's not like the county isn't lousy with Taskers. Maybe a cousin decided to make an investment and you were just caught in the cross fire."

"Investment? Have you been to downtown Bell Grove lately?" she asked, but her voice was low. Her face had returned to a somewhat normal color. "Besides, Martin was so excited that someone was paying more than the land was worth, he all but danced into my shop to share the news."

It was an odd situation, he'd give her that, but at the moment he could only concentrate on one thing: she'd been given the opportunity to think the worst of him, and that's exactly what she'd done.

"If I was going to buy that building in an attempt to run you out of town, to come in here like some lousy white knight and create my own opportunity to rescue you, you can be assured that I could manage to do so without the Tasker name being involved. I could rip that building out from under you and you would never have a clue that I was the buyer. I'd run it through so many lawyers and companies that it would take a *very* long time to sort out the details. You'd never know. Chestnut would never know. Not that I'm so desperate for you to come with me that I'd try to force you into that position. Do I look desperate, Daisy?"

"No." There was a hint of concession in her voice.

He took another step forward; she matched him with a step back.

"No," he repeated. "I was hoping you would decide to come home with me of your own free will, I was hoping it might be a choice you'd gladly make. Judging by the look on your face, I was wrong." Judging by the look on her face, she was furious not only that someone had bought the building she leased, but that she might have to leave Bell Grove. He'd been right about that all along. Daisy belonged in Bell Grove. She wasn't going anywhere.

"I don't know what I want anymore," Daisy said.

"I was hoping you might want me."

She shook her head. "I did. I do. Dammit, Jacob, I'm so

angry right now, I'm so hurt and confused. I don't know what comes next."

He stepped back, picked up his bag and turned around, glad that he couldn't see the pained expression on her face anymore. Glad that she couldn't see his.

"I'll find out who's behind this," he said as he walked down the steps. "I'll let you know." So much for taking Daisy home with him. So much for seeing how things worked out for them. If she was so quick to condemn him without even asking a single question, if she really thought so little of him, they didn't have a chance.

It was dark out when the doorbell rang. Daisy jumped. Surely Jacob hadn't come back! If it really wasn't him who'd bought the building out from under her, and he'd found out who had, he would've just called. She hadn't missed the fury in his eyes as she'd accused him. She couldn't possibly have misread the way he'd closed off, shut down.

She still didn't know who else might've done it, but she'd believed Jacob when he'd said it wasn't him. Too late. He'd never forgive her for doubting him, and if she was so quick to believe the worst maybe that was just as well. All they had was a bit of history and great sex. Neither was enough to build a lasting relationship upon.

When she peeked through the security viewer, she sighed in relief. Then she opened the door and asked, "What on earth are you doing here?"

Lily Bell had always been the difficult middle child. If there was a disagreement to be had, she was right in the middle of it. She'd argue any point just for the sake of arguing. There had been a while, a tough while, when her idea of a good time had included too much beer and staying out all night. For the past several years she'd dyed her dark blond hair black—or red or platinum, though it was normally black and it was black tonight—because she wanted to be different from her sisters.

She didn't have to dye her hair to be different. Lily had always been edgier than her sisters. Tougher, through and through. And at the moment, she was steaming.

"Those bastards," Lily said as she walked inside. Then she explained. "Mari called and told me what was going on. She can't miss class tomorrow or Friday, so I took the rest of the week off and drove up." Hands on hips, she asked. "Why didn't you call me? I mean, the first call was fine. Getting out of the business, selling the house, blah, blah, blah. But the second call, the one I didn't get? The Taskers?"

"I know you're busy with the new job," Daisy explained weakly. "I didn't want to bother you."

Lily responded by giving Daisy a big hug. "It's never a bother to hear from you. We're family. We stick together." She kept her hands on Daisy's shoulders as she pulled away. "Do you have a plan?"

Daisy shook her head. A plan? She still wasn't sure what she was going to do about dinner Friday night! Miss Vivian was expecting a dinner at the Tasker House with her old friend and rival, but if Daisy didn't fix her hair and take her she wouldn't go. And the old woman might never get another chance.

"Well, *I* have a plan." Lily plopped down on the couch. "At first I was just furious, but on the drive up I did some thinking. You sell the house like you planned, and come stay with me. Screw the Taskers. They can buy all of downtown Bell Grove for all I care, and they can choke on it. Go back to school, Daisy, or better yet take a job styling hair in Atlanta…"

"I can't work in Atlanta! The competition there is…"

"You're as good as any of them," Lily said. "Better than most. I know styling hair isn't what you planned to do when you went to school, but you're good at it and I think you like it. Why do you think I drive all the way to Bell Grove to get my hair cut?"

"Because I don't charge you?"

Lily laughed. "Okay, there is that. But if you weren't the best I'd pay someone else to do it and save the gas money."

"I don't know…" Daisy sat beside her sister. It was nice, not to be alone with her out-of-control thoughts and regrets.

"Maybe this is a blessing," Lily said, sounding oddly calm and reasonable.

"How can you say that?"

Lily looked Daisy in the eye. "You're stuck here, you're in a rut. Face it, Daisy, you don't belong in Bell Grove anymore. What are you going to do here, even if you stay and find another location for the shop? Keep on running Mom and Dad's business, make enough to get by and eventually marry some local guy. Though, honestly, I can't think of a single man in town who's good enough for you. If you move to Atlanta you'll have so many more options. You can start over. The world is so much bigger than Bell Grove, Daisy, and you need to be a part of it. It's time."

Time. Past time. "Will you miss it?" she asked, watching Lily's face for a clue to her feelings.

"Miss what?"

"The shop, the house…" She almost choked on the words. "What's left of Mom and Dad. Once it's all gone there won't be any getting that back."

"Oh, Daisy." Lily leaned in for a hug. "Of course I'll miss it. But nothing stays the same, and it's been such a long time. Is that why you stayed here? Please tell me you didn't stay for us, for me and Mari."

"No, I stayed for myself, because I couldn't let what

was left of them go. I didn't even realize it until a few hours ago."

Daisy had been furious. Before that she'd been shocked, and sad, and relieved and hopeful. All in the space of a few hours. Talking to Jacob had settled her down some, even though their conversation hadn't ended on a happy note. Now Lily opened her eyes to options she hadn't considered. A spark of excitement grew where her fear had been. Everything and everyone in Bell Grove was familiar to her. She was safe here, and she felt her parents' presence everywhere. It had been comfortable, but it hadn't been right. She knew that, now.

It was time to set safety aside in the name of moving on. Not with Jacob, not to the other side of the country, but moving on just the same.

Daisy rested her head on Lily's shoulder. "I'm glad you came."

"Me, too."

Lily's voice brightened. "Now that we have that settled, who do we kill first?"

Jacob didn't see anyone when he entered the house, but he was sure they could hear him. He didn't try to be quiet, didn't soften the slam of the door behind him. He walked up the stairs to his bedroom, opened the door, threw his bag onto the floor and headed for the closet and his cell phone.

With a flick of his thumb he turned it on, and within seconds the icons for voice mail messages and texts popped up. He didn't have time to listen to or read a single message, not now. Maybe later, when he couldn't sleep. Jacob was pretty sure he wouldn't be sleeping tonight. He was too wound up, too disappointed. It was three hours earlier in San Francisco, and he knew Ted would still be in the office.

Ted didn't have a personal life any more than Jacob did. He dialed on a direct line, and Ted answered.

As soon as Jacob spoke, Ted interrupted and began his rant. "Where the hell have you been! Hudson's been calling you, and he's furious that you haven't called him back."

"Hudson's always furious," Jacob said. "And I'm on vacation. I need a favor."

"A favor. You leave me here all alone..."

"You're hardly alone."

"It feels like I'm alone when they expect me to do your job *and* mine. So, what's it like to be on vacation? It's been so long I don't really remember."

"You should try it sometime. Now, about that favor. I need you to track down the purchaser of a particular property here in Bell Grove."

"You can't do that from your end?"

"Eventually, but with your connections through the office you should be able to find out details quicker than I can. Besides, I have my hands full here." Between Daisy and Grandma Eunice and the upcoming reunion...Jacob had to wonder how any man managed to balance a demanding job with a family.

"Blonde, brunette or redhead?" Ted asked with a smile in his voice.

Definitely blonde. But instead of responding to the question aloud, Jacob told Ted what he knew about the sale that had ripped Daisy's business out from under her. Daisy hadn't even considered that the name Tasker had been dropped like a bomb, when in fact no one from the family was involved. Someone was trying to set him up. Why?

Daisy had been so quick to believe that it was him, that he'd stoop so low to get what he wanted. Her. She didn't have a very high opinion of him if she truly believed he'd manipulate her that way. After the way things had ended last time, maybe she had good reason. He'd chosen his career over her and Bell Grove. And he did do whatever was necessary to get what he wanted. But before he left town he wanted to make sure she knew he wasn't the one who'd bought a chunk of downtown and run her out of business. For all the good that would do him.

Jacob realized with a sinking heart he'd be leaving town alone, when the reunion was over and he'd done his duty to the family. But when he left Daisy would know without a doubt that he hadn't been the one to force her out of the building where her family's business had been operating for twenty-plus years.

Would she feel at all guilty when he proved himself innocent, or would she just be glad to see him go?

Chapter Thirteen

Lily hadn't bothered to pack much for her trip. The overnight bag she'd brought with her had some toiletries and a pair of pajamas. When Daisy asked, Lily said she had more than enough clothes in her old closet. They were going to have to talk about that, Daisy decided, thinking about the dress that had shocked the Taskers and driven Jacob into overdrive. Lily had never been shy, she loved the shock factor, but some of her clothing choices were outrageous.

They were too busy on Wednesday night to talk much about plans, but as Daisy cut and styled hair Thursday, and Lily made a Going Out Of Business sign and called customers who'd left things behind to be repaired and had never picked them up, Daisy's mind spun wildly.

Bell Grove was her safety net; this shop was her parachute. She was comfortable here, so comfortable she'd stopped growing. Now that she realized what she'd been doing by trying to keep her parents' memories vibrant by living their lives, it seemed so obvious. And so wrong. Maybe that's the reason Jacob had seemed so attractive to her, for a while. He had been a way out. Nothing more.

In between customers and friends who saw the sign and stopped by, she and Lily made plans. Lily's Atlanta apartment was a two-bedroom, two-bath, so no problem there—though she did note that eventually Daisy would want her own place. Having a big sister around would seriously cramp Lily's style. Lily had already chosen a couple of men she thought were Daisy's type, and had been talking about blind dates. These were men she'd rejected, most likely, though she didn't say so. Daisy didn't even want to think about men, but Lily was already talking about double dates, making plans for nights out in Atlanta.

Which made Daisy think of her date with Jacob, and how foolish she'd been to believe for a minute that they had something more. At the moment she couldn't even imagine dating another man, much less getting involved in a serious relationship. Apparently she didn't do relationships well. Maybe she was destined to be the spinster sister, always alone, watching while her sisters moved on with their lives and she remained stagnant.

The opposite mindset from the one she'd been searching for when she'd allowed herself to get involved with Jacob Tasker again.

At the end of the day, she and Lily walked home together. Daisy was still sad about Jacob, sorry she'd accused him of being the one to buy the building and still not a hundred percent sure he hadn't been involved, even though she wanted to believe him. Obviously she didn't trust him enough to pick up where they'd left off seven years ago. The sex was great, but it was all they had. How could she love him and like him and need him and not trust him? What was *wrong* with her?

Atlanta was sounding better and better. She'd get away, start fresh and leave behind this little town where she felt safe. Here she was sheltered from the outside world. She didn't want to be sheltered anymore.

But apparently she was not averse to running away...

Lily was preparing dinner when Daisy decided to call Jacob. It wouldn't be easy, but she needed to talk to him. No matter what had happened, they needed a plan. Miss Eunice, Miss Vivian...all the plans they'd made that involved more than the two of them...she couldn't just walk away. Naturally he didn't answer the phone, and Susan—who'd answered with a formal "Tasker residence"—was less than cordial. No surprise, there.

It didn't take Jacob long to get to the phone, and when he spoke his voice was cool.

"I've been thinking about tomorrow," Daisy said, trying for a nonchalant voice. "I don't want to disappoint Miss Vivian, and we do have your grandmother to think of, so I suppose one more dinner is in order."

He agreed.

"And after dinner, we will tell Miss Eunice that we're not going to get married." *Not now, not ever.*

"It won't take," he said sharply. "Trust me, I've tried."

"Maybe if we tell her together she'll understand."

After a short pause, he said, "We can try."

She paused herself, for a long moment. "I know I said I'd help, and I do feel so bad about the situation with your grandmother, but we need to make the truth stick. Somehow." She took a deep breath. This should be easy, but it wasn't. "I'm not sure how much longer I'm going to be in town. I hope to be gone by the time the Tasker Reunion rolls around."

"Where are you going?" His voice was emotionless, distant.

"To Atlanta, with Lily. With the shop closing…"

"The shop doesn't have to close," he interrupted sharply. "I'm trying to find out who's behind the sale, and then… dammit, Daisy, I'll buy the place myself so you can stay. You don't have to run away."

"I'm not running away," she argued without heat, denying the accusation even though she'd had the same thought. "Not really. I'm moving forward. It's time. To be honest it's very much past time."

"Is that what you want?" His voice was crisp, distant. Was this the same man who'd whispered in her ear, held her, danced?

"Yes."

"All right, then."

"Dinner tomorrow," Daisy said as she prepared to hang up. "The regular time?"

Lily called out from the kitchen. "Tell them to set another plate. There's no way in hell I'd miss this shindig." She should've known her sister had been eavesdropping.

"Did you hear that?" Daisy asked.

"I'll make sure a place is set for your sister. It'll be a big night. Caleb is arriving tomorrow, too."

"The more the merrier, I suppose." Daisy wanted to tell Jacob that she was sorry, that she'd made a terrible mistake…and she would. But not over the phone. And not when he sounded like he was already more than two thousand miles away.

Caleb arrived shortly after lunchtime, parking his pickup truck next to Jacob's rental car. Dressed in jeans that had seen better days and in need of a shave, he made his way reluctantly to the front door. Those long legs could take much longer steps. He didn't have to look as if he were marching to the electric chair!

Eunice watched from her window. Caleb had so much potential. He'd had a good education, but he'd wasted his knowledge on starting a small construction company. A Tasker, working with his hands! Caleb was no dummy, she knew that, but he was as stubborn as the day was long.

He needed a wife himself, one more suitable than the first bimbo he'd been married to for a few weeks. When she was finished with Jacob she'd fix Caleb's life for him. First a decent job, then an appropriate wife.

Eunice felt as if she were the hub of a creaking wheel that was on the verge of falling apart. Three of her four grandsons were so far away; they had separated themselves from the family. And Ben…bless him, he tried hard, and he had remained near home and with the company, but he didn't have the strength to hold the family together when she was gone. Jim…well, she'd given up on her son long ago. He wasn't exactly a wastrel, but he didn't miss the mark by much. The future of this family rested squarely on the shoulders of her grandsons.

Maybe she was faking this latest illness, but Eunice was very well aware that she wouldn't live forever. She had a few good years left, God willing, and she wanted to see her family solidly knit together before she left this world.

First Jacob…then Caleb. She wondered if he'd be as cooperative as his younger brother.

Daisy tried to convince herself that this would be easier than it had been so far. Knowing that she wouldn't be here much longer, knowing there wasn't a drop of truth in the charade, should make playing the part of Jacob's bride-to-be a little less painful. Oh, she still wanted him, she still yearned for him in a place she tried very hard to deny, but now she knew that when he left—again—she wouldn't be staying behind. She'd be moving on, too. There would be no time for moping.

Away from Bell Grove she'd be able to completely leave the past behind. She wouldn't be reminded of Jacob Tasker everywhere she looked. She'd have a new life, in a new place, where she'd meet new people and make a new home. It was a little scary, she'd admit, but it was also exciting. With Lily there she wouldn't be entirely on her own, so she'd have the best of both worlds.

She'd been working toward a degree in elementary education, seven years ago, and she *could* go back to school. But after suffering through hundreds of children's haircuts, she wasn't sure teaching was the career for her. She could pick a new field of study, or do as Lily suggested and try her luck as a hairdresser in a more competitive market.

The world was wide-open; her life was unplanned.

Lily let Miss Vivian have the front seat; she happily climbed into the back. Vivian's hair was brushed and braided and twisted. Lily had insisted on applying a little bit of makeup, and the older woman had not protested. She wore a Sunday dress, squat black pumps and pearls. Daisy was surprised; she'd never seen Miss Vivian wear any jewelry other than her wedding ring. She looked downright respectable, every inch the proper Southern lady.

As they drove toward Tasker House, Daisy gently told Miss Vivian how she and Jacob were pretending to be engaged to placate Eunice. She should've done it sooner, but it wasn't an easy thing to explain! Vivian was shocked to hear that her old friend—and enemy—had degenerated to such a point. She was silent after that, thoughtful as she stared out the passenger window.

Lily wasn't at all silent. She never was. She talked about Atlanta, the apartment, selling the house. As they turned onto the long driveway with Tasker House at the end, Miss Vivian turned to look—no, to *glare*—at Daisy.

"You're moving to Atlanta?"

Lily answered. "She doesn't have much of a choice. Some Tasker bought the building out from under her."

"There are other buildings," Vivian argued.

It was Lily who responded. "Yeah, but it would be a hassle to move, and there would be expenses involved in getting a new place set up, and besides, Daisy needs to get out of Bell Grove."

Daisy added. "I'll come visit you, Miss Vivian. Atlanta isn't all that far away."

The old lady huffed, and looked out the window again. Her chin came up defiantly, and her voice was harsher than it had been. "You won't visit. Oh, maybe you'll make it to town once or twice, not long after you move away, but eventually you'll stop coming."

"I won't," Daisy insisted.

"You'll escape this little town and you won't look back. I don't blame you. I should've gotten out years ago." She turned and stared at Daisy. "Good for you, girlie. I'll miss you, but it's past time you got out of this place."

"See, Daisy?" Lily said brightly. "I told you so."

Daisy didn't respond. She knew leaving town was right, she knew a better life was waiting for her. But a boulder of doubt had settled in her gut and it wouldn't go away.

The dining room was crowded tonight. Jacob and Caleb, their parents, Ben and Maddy, Daisy and her sister Lily—who kept glaring in Jacob's direction and had even stuck her tongue out once, when she'd thought no one else was looking. Vivian Reynolds was there, too, looking very different from the wild-haired, plain woman who'd pointed a shotgun in his direction earlier in the week. She cleaned up well and looked downright respectable.

Lurlene wheeled Grandma Eunice into the room. The family matriarch made a grand entrance, which she very much enjoyed. As usual. Her eyes scanned the room, lingering for a moment on Lily. She frowned as introductions were made, but recovered quickly, perhaps realizing that she needed to be welcoming to Daisy's sister, even if Lily did have a reputation as a bit of a wild child.

Then she looked at Vivian, puzzled for a moment. After that moment, recognition showed on her face in shock and even horror. "Dear God, what are *you* doing here?"

"Miss Eunice," Daisy said sweetly, "I thought you might enjoy seeing an old friend again."

"An old friend? Is that what you think—" She stopped short, raised a hand to her forehead and blinked quickly several times. "Who are you?" she asked Vivian. "You do look vaguely familiar."

Vivian smiled oddly and took her seat. "We used to go fishing together, many years ago." She remained calm. Of course, she'd been forewarned about her old friend's mental condition.

"I don't fish," Eunice responded coldly. "Fishing is for men and small boys. Ladies do not fish."

"Well, you once did." Vivian smiled at the hostess. "Susan, this meal looks just wonderful. It's very gracious of you to have me." She hardly looked, or sounded, like the harridan who had threatened him with a shotgun and called his grandmother an "old bitch."

Tonight, after dinner, he and Daisy would break the bad news to Eunice. They weren't engaged. They never had been. It wasn't going to be easy. Throughout dinner Grandma Eunice ignored everyone but Daisy. She talked about wedding plans—the wedding was just a week away!—the dress Daisy still hadn't tried on, food for the reunion and the wedding reception. Everyone but Vivian, who was thoughtfully quiet throughout, tried to change the subject. The weather, the cousins who would be coming in the following weekend, sports, recipes. But there was no swaying the very determined woman.

Grandma Eunice wanted to talk about the brides-maids—Daisy's sisters, she assumed, looking pointedly at Lily as she suggested matching yellow gowns. Reverend Ashton would perform the ceremony, of course. Grandma Eunice said she'd already ordered the cake, and mentioned who was going to take care of that task. Jacob made a mental note to call the cake maker first thing in the morning. Monday, if they were closed on Saturday. The last thing he needed was a tiered wedding cake showing up during the reunion.

When that was done and Grandma Eunice sighed in satisfaction, Vivian and Lily turned the conversation around. Finally. They drew Caleb into their discussion, asking about his business in Macon. Lily talked about her new job, about life in Atlanta…though she did know better than to mention that her sister would soon be joining her there. Maddy added in her two cents; she loved Atlanta, loved the shopping there and thought that Lily's job at an art gallery sounded very cool.

Daisy didn't say much at all. Neither did Jacob. He was having a hard time choking down much in the way of dinner, and judging by the way Daisy played with the food on her plate, maybe she had a lump in her throat like the one that had formed—and stayed—in his.

Jacob never suffered this way at home, in San Francisco. He never felt as if the world around him was spinning wildly and there wasn't a damn thing he could do.

There was still a week until the family reunion began.

A full week. Jacob was suddenly anxious to get back to work, back to a world he knew and could manage. Here everything was out of control; including him. He wanted Daisy; he missed having her in his life. But she'd proved that she didn't trust him, and they couldn't have a long lasting relationship without trust.

Maybe he'd lost the right to expect her trust years ago.

Maybe he'd never deserved it.

Daisy didn't look forward to telling Miss Eunice the truth, but it had to be done. She'd agreed to this farce in order to placate the delusional woman, but she was having second thoughts over a difficult dinner. Had she just made matters worse by playing along thus far? Would finding out that there would be no wedding at the Tasker Reunion send the matriarch into a downward spiral? She didn't want to be responsible for causing problems, but the truth of the matter was, she might not be here for the Tasker Reunion. Not that she'd ever planned to let this ridiculous scheme go that far.

They would break the news gently, and then Daisy would leave and Jacob would be left behind to deal with the fallout. Daisy looked at Caleb, who sat directly across from her. Why hadn't Miss Eunice fixated on him? He was older than Jacob, lived closer—though from what she'd heard he didn't make it home often. Maybe he needed a little polishing, but there might be a gem in there. Somewhere.

As dessert was served—a choice of strawberry or chocolate cake—Miss Vivian launched into another tale of the old days. Miss Eunice just looked confused, as if she had no idea what the other woman was talking about. Fishing. Hikes in the woods. Skipping school.

Miss Eunice fanned herself with her napkin as if she

were suddenly warm, and even said, at one point, that their guest must have her confused with someone else.

And then Miss Vivian put her fork down, took a sip of her decaffeinated coffee and looked squarely at Miss Eunice. "Have you ever told your family about the time you pretended to sprain your ankle to get my fella to carry you home?"

Miss Eunice sputtered. "I have no idea what you're talking about."

Vivian laughed. "Come on, Eunice. It's been more than sixty years and you have the same tells when you lie. You drum your fingers and your right eyelid twitches. You cock your head to the left." Miss Vivian turned to Daisy and glared with strong, certain eyes. "You *do* know she's lying about the memory lapses, don't you?"

Chapter Fourteen

Everyone at the table went silent and still. For a long moment you could've heard a pin drop. Then Caleb coughed, and Lily put a hand over her mouth and muttered a soft, "Oh, my God."

Jacob stared at his grandmother and tried to recall how often he'd seen the "tells" Vivian spoke of, since he'd returned home. He would dismiss the bitter old woman's accusations as a mean-spirited joke, if not for the expression on Eunice Tasker's face.

She was horrified. Chastened. Guilty. *Caught*. Those fleeting expressions didn't last long. She tried to recover and insist that she had no idea what their guest was talking about, but it was too late for proclamations of innocence. It didn't help matters at all that as Grandma Eunice pretended to be ignorant, her eyelid twitched. She tried to catch the telling tilt of the head—a half second too late—and she clutched at the armrests of her wheelchair, apparently to keep her fingers from tapping.

"Miss Eunice?" Daisy said softly. Even she—who was so willing to look for the good in everyone but him—could see the truth, now. The color drained from her cheeks. "Did you really...all this time...oh, my God, it makes a sick kind of sense." Tears welled up in her eyes. "That's why you never spoke of my parents as if they were still alive, even though when Jacob and I were together they were still with us. You couldn't bring yourself to be *that* cruel." She pushed away from the table, stood and ran out of the room without looking back. Lily followed.

Jacob started to rise and follow, but he didn't. Not yet. Daisy hadn't been happy with him when the evening had started; she surely didn't want anything to do with him now.

Maddy looked from her husband to her mother-in-law to the matriarch. It took her a moment but soon she, too, stood. She did *not* cry as she directed her attention to her husband's grandmother. "So all this time you've been pretending you didn't remember me, when you've been mistaking me for a cook or a seamstress or a maid, it was a *joke?* You have got to be kidding me," she added under her breath as she threw her napkin to the table.

She left the room, storming out with her head held high and her husband on her heels. Ben shot one last glance at his grandmother. Jacob read the shock on his brother's face, the disbelief and condemnation.

"Really, Mother?" Jim Tasker said, sounding both resigned and sad. It was telling that he didn't sound particularly surprised.

Maybe if she'd been prepared for the bombshell, Grandma Eunice would've handled the situation better. But as it was she sat there, guilt written all over her face. She didn't say a word in her own defense, didn't attempt to pretend that she had no idea what everyone was talking about. She hadn't been losing her mind; she was sharp as a tack and as ruthless as ever.

Susan put her palms on the table and took a deep breath. In an instant she left behind her role as hostess and became the woman who'd taken on the family business affairs as if she'd been born to them. The fixer, a level head the family could rely on. "This revelation is distressing, that's true, but the reunion starts next weekend and we *will* move on and get past this. No one outside this room has to know…"

Jacob finally stood. "I won't be here for the reunion." He didn't feel the need to say anything more as he left the room.

At the moment he longed for an uncomplicated life filled with work and nothing else. He longed for a schedule he could follow; command and control over the events that ruled his days.

But most of all, he longed for Daisy, and after this… after this he figured there was no way she'd ever speak to a Tasker again.

He couldn't say he blamed her.

"You battle-ax," Eunice said sharply as Vivian rose and stepped in her direction. "How dare you come into my home and interfere in family concerns? Can you see what you've done? You've ruined everything."

Those few who remained in the dining room were talking among themselves, ignoring her as they discussed potential ways to fix the damage she'd done. At least, that was the way they phrased it. Eunice didn't see that she'd done any damage. All she'd done was put Jacob and Daisy together so they could find their way. That wasn't so bad. Was it?

Susan moved to Jim's side and put her hand on his shoulder. Jim patted Susan's hand then left his hand sit-

ting there, on hers. Funny, but she didn't see them this
way often. Together. United. Good heavens, different as
they were—imperfect as they were—they were still in
love. Maybe her son had done something right, after all.

Jim and Susan, even Caleb, talked about the reunion,
Doc Porter and all those who had left the dining room
table with hurt feelings.

Eunice only felt guilty about one of them. Daisy.

"What *I've* done?" Vivian repeated. "I told the truth.
Not that you'd recognize the truth even if it bit you on that
overly generous ass of yours."

Eunice gasped. How dare this woman come into her
home, disrupt all her plans and then insult her? She tried
to come up with a proper response, but words failed her.
She hadn't had time to plan for this, to mull over her words,
to script the evening.

"You're the one who's been lying to your family, Eunice. You're the one who has once again woven a tale in
order to get your way." Vivian leaned over and gripped
the handles of the wheelchair Eunice sat in. "Do you even
need this contraption? I can just see you, using the wheelchair to get sympathy, then getting up at night and walking around the house when no one else can…"

"I do need this chair, dammit. I wish I didn't."

Vivian placed herself behind the wheelchair and pulled
Eunice sharply away from the table. Eunice gripped the
armrests and screamed weakly for help. Vivian—her oldest friend, her oldest rival—stopped and looked toward
Susan, rightly sizing her up as the one in charge.

"I'll just take her to her room, if that suits you. Y'all
have work to do and I don't think Eunice will be of much
help here, given the circumstances."

Susan agreed, dismissing Eunice without giving much
thought to the obvious peril she was putting her mother-

in-law in. The hateful woman who had ruined everything might decide to push an old, helpless woman down the front porch steps, or dump her in the hallway and leave her there to flounder and call for help that wouldn't come. Panic welled up and she gripped the armrests of her wheelchair and held on. For the first time in a very long time, she was not in charge of the situation.

"Where to?" Vivian asked as she pushed the wheelchair into the wide hallway.

Eunice pointed, half expecting Vivian to turn in the opposite direction out of spite. That didn't happen.

Vivian pushed the chair slowly, even gently. She sighed. "If I was lucky enough to have a family, I wouldn't lie to them," she said. "You should be ashamed of yourself."

That truth hurt, even though Eunice was still convinced she'd done the right thing. Jacob needed Daisy. If not for the very necessary lies she'd told of late, he'd still be in San Francisco! Didn't the end justify the means? That wasn't a discussion she intended to have with this interloper. "Surely you have some family, somewhere."

"No." There was sadness in Vivian's voice. "Frank and I never had children. I had two miscarriages, and after that I just didn't get pregnant. There are a few nieces and nephews scattered about, but we were never close. I doubt they even know I'm still alive."

"I'm sorry," Eunice said. "I lost three myself…two stillborn before Jim and one who died at a few days old when Jim was three." She thought about how nice it would've been to have the support of a friend in those tough times. She wondered if Vivian had had a friend to help her when she'd lost her babies. There was no way to describe that pain to someone who had not been there.

Claiming the man she'd loved had cost her a good

friend. She'd thought the trade a fair one, at the time. Now she was not so sure.

The past was still between them, a living thing after all this time. "I loved him," Eunice whispered. "You had Charles, for a while, but you never truly loved him. Not like I did."

"I know." Vivian stopped pushing, positioned Eunice, set the brake and walked around the wheelchair to sit in the occasional chair in the hallway. Now they were face-to-face, and for the first time Eunice looked her old friend in the eye without lies between them. Vivian was a strong old bird, stringy and wrinkled and healthy, for her age. She wore a life of hardship on her face; it was clear in her eyes that she had struggled. And yet the face was still much the same. Eunice saw the girl she remembered in those eyes, in the set of the mouth. "But he was still mine, and you took him."

"If it makes you feel better, I don't think he ever entirely got over you."

Vivian smiled. "That does make me feel a little better."

"Not that he didn't love *me*," Eunice felt compelled to point out.

Vivian waved that statement off with a dismissive gesture of her hand. "We can talk about the past later, if it suits us to do so. For now, we need to fix this mess you've made."

"May I point out that there would not be a mess to fix if you had kept your mouth shut?" Eunice couldn't help it that her voice was sharp. As far as she could see, Vivian had ruined a perfectly good scheme.

"You may, but that's not the case. Your ridiculous plan wasn't working."

"What do you mean it wasn't working?" It had been working perfectly!

"On the way here Daisy told me that she's moving to Atlanta to live with her sister. Is that what you had in mind?"

Eunice pursed her lips. "No."

"I didn't think so. Daisy is crazy about that grandson of yours, and he's definitely got a thing for her. We can't let this mess you've made pull them apart."

"We?"

Vivian sighed. "Maybe I should've kept my mouth shut, but you were so obvious I just couldn't do it."

"I wasn't obvious to anyone else."

"They don't know you the way I do." Vivian stood, kicked off the brake and righted the wheelchair. "Your room?"

Eunice pointed. Before they could enter the room, Lurlene came around the corner, moving as quickly as possible, for her old bones.

"Lurlene, thank goodness you're here," Eunice said dramatically.

Vivian sighed and stopped pushing.

Eunice caught Lurlene's eye. She could have Vivian kicked out of the house. It was her house after all. But even though there were things to be settled between them, she was very aware that life was moving quickly by, and she didn't have many friends left. She didn't have any as close as Vivian had once been, and none of them would dare to buck her.

"I'll need six chocolate covered cherries tonight, three for me and three for my friend. Vivian, would you like another cup of decaf? Perhaps some tea?"

There was a moment's hesitation before Vivian answered. "Sure. Decaf. Cream and sugar, please."

"So tell me," Eunice said as Vivian wheeled her into her suite. "How can we fix this?"

* * *

Daisy ran. Out of the dining room, out of the house, past the cars parked by the front porch. She kept running, realizing on some level that Lily was right behind her. Lily didn't try to catch up to her sister. She could have, but instead she kept a short distance between them. She was close, in case she was needed, but far enough away to allow Daisy to have some privacy.

Daisy knew she could turn and run into her sister's arms, she could pour out all her fears and anger and frustration. But she was unable to speak…unable to stop running. She ran up a gentle hill toward the cover of trees that were in stark contrast to the brilliant colors the setting sun had left behind.

At the base of an old oak tree, she stopped. She was out of breath and her legs shook from the effort. She put her hands on the trunk, leaned forward and took a deep breath. For a moment she thought she might throw up, but she didn't. Her stomach pitched and rolled, and her heart pounded—from the run and more.

She was such an idiot! A gullible fool. She hated the Taskers, each and every one of them. If she never saw a Tasker again it would be too soon.

Lily placed a comforting hand on her back, and with that touch tears came. Daisy didn't want to cry, but she did. The tears that ran down her cheeks weren't tears of sadness; they were tears of anger.

Getting out of town seemed even more attractive than it had before. Attractive? Hell, it was *necessary*.

Then Lily asked the question that had been plaguing Daisy. "Do you think Jacob knew all along?"

It was her greatest fear, that Jacob really had been playing with her from the moment he'd stepped into her shop, that it had all been a game. But she'd seen the look on his face when Miss Vivian dropped the bombshell. She didn't think a single person at that table had realized what was going on. If any one of them did, they were a great actor.

"No," she whispered, sniffling. "I don't think he knew. I think Miss Eunice lied to get him home, and then she lied to try to force us together." If she'd thought Jacob was involved, if she believed for one second that he'd been in on the ruse, she'd never recover. She'd never trust anyone again. "How the hell far was she willing to go?"

"All the way, I'm guessing," Lily said, her voice sharp.

Daisy turned, leaned her back against the tree trunk and slid down into a sitting position. She didn't have the strength to stand, at the moment. Her knees were knocking; her heart was beating too hard. She wiped away her tears, angry at herself for allowing them to fall in the first place.

She was going to have to find strength, and she'd need it for more than standing and walking away. She was going to have to find the strength to start a new life, say goodbye to Jacob, say goodbye to everything she knew. At the moment, escape sounded really good. More than good, she was coming to accept that escaping from Bell Grove, a home she truly loved, was necessary.

Lily sat down in front of Daisy, crossed her legs and leaned forward. "You can't let one old bat's sick game send you into a tailspin."

"What makes you think I'm…"

"You're pale, your hands are shaking, you're crying, and instead of heading for the car when the truth came out you kept running. In case you haven't noticed that we're sitting in the middle of nowhere."

Daisy stared at her sister in the dying light. "I'm not as strong as you are."

Lily's response was a single word that would've shocked

their parents. It even shocked Daisy, a little. "You're the strongest of us all. You're a rock for me and Mari, and you always have been. There was a time I almost hated you for being so damn perfect."

Daisy snorted. She was so *not* perfect.

"It's true," Lily snapped. "You gave up everything for us, and don't think we don't realize that. Mari and I never wanted for anything after Mom and Dad died, we had a stable home, food on the table, clothes. More than that, we still had a family. Thanks to you. That's strength, Daisy."

She leaned forward, and so did Lily. They hugged, tight.

"You really are the strongest person I know," Lily whispered.

And in the distance she heard a frustrated Jacob calling her name.

Chapter Fifteen

Her car was parked right where she'd left it, but where was Daisy? Jacob circled the house. As soon as complete darkness fell he'd have a hell of a time finding her and worse, she'd have a hell of a time finding her way back, if she'd wandered far. He checked out the garage and the gardens. Nothing.

The look on her face as the truth sank in and took hold had broken his heart. And he was to blame. He hadn't lied to her, he hadn't purposely hurt her, but he'd dragged her into this charade that had hurt her so badly. Where would she go, if she didn't jump in the car and make a quick escape?

After searching the immediate property as thoroughly as he could without a flashlight, Jacob rounded the house to the front, again. Daisy's car was still here. She wasn't in it, and neither was Lily. She couldn't have gone far. In frustration he shouted her name. Would that call her to him, or scare her away?

Jacob was embarrassed and angry; he felt as if he'd been betrayed. So how did Daisy feel right now? Wherever she might be, he imagined she was experiencing all of the same emotions. And more.

If she hadn't hated him before tonight, she did now. Not that he'd known what his grandmother had been up to, not that he would ever condone that kind of trickery, but still…he was a Tasker, and the head of the clan had screwed Daisy over in a big way.

After a few very long minutes, movement caught his eye. Finally! Two women—Daisy and her sister—approached from the west. They didn't seem to be in a hurry. Dusk made a colorful pastel backdrop for them as they headed slowly in his direction. Skirts fluttered in the breeze, and as they came closer and saw him standing there, Lily reached out and took Daisy's hand.

Comfort offered because he was close.

Jacob was glad Daisy had her sisters; he was grateful to know they would always be there for her. He wished he could be the one to comfort her, wished she would let him take her hand in tough times. And good times, too.

When they reached him, Lily shot daggers his way with her dark eyes. Daisy turned and dipped her head and whispered something to her sister, and Lily reluctantly released Daisy's hand and headed for the steps, a path that took her right past Jacob. As she brushed by him she muttered, "Addams family."

He ignored her. She had every right to be angry.

"I'm so sorry," he said when he and Daisy were alone. "I didn't have any idea what she'd done."

"I know," Daisy said, her voice so low he could barely hear her. "Everyone at the table looked so surprised. This mess appears to be all your grandmother's doings. Maybe she really is unwell, just not the way we thought."

"Maybe. Personally I think she's just a world-class control freak and she wanted what she wanted and would do anything to get it." His words were sharp, condemning. And, he was certain, right.

Daisy nodded. "That's probably so. I suppose I'd prefer to think that a woman I once admired was sick, rather than cruel and manipulative. All evidence to the contrary," she whispered. She lifted her head and looked him in the eye. "So, are you still sticking around for the reunion?"

"I don't think so." He walked toward her, but the way her body stiffened when he moved in her direction stopped him from closing the gap between them. He wouldn't do anything to make her more uncomfortable. He wouldn't stay for his family, but he'd stay for her, if she asked him to. What were the odds of that happening? Slim to none, he figured.

"I don't have any proof, but I suppose it was your grandmother who bought my downtown space."

He would have proof soon, if Ted did his job. "I'd guess so. No matter who it was, I can make it right for you. I can stop the deal before…"

"Don't," Daisy said sharply. "She can have it. Martin wants to retire, and it's a good deal for him. Besides, I'm not staying in this town, no matter what."

His heart sank, a little. Bell Grove without Daisy in it was just wrong. He didn't have the right to try to change her mind. "You're going to Atlanta with Lily?"

She nodded. "Not right away. I still have to finish cleaning out the shop, and there will be papers to sign to get the house on the market. Someone will have to replace me on my Monday meals run, and…well, there are a million small details to take care of before I go."

She looked so vulnerable, so sad. He didn't think she really wanted to leave Bell Grove: she was being forced out of town. He felt helpless, and he was angry for her. His mother had been right; he'd just been slow to accept the truth. He did still love her. Not the same way he'd loved her years ago, not in a way he could explain. But there it was. Too late.

Maybe not too late. If Daisy knew that he still loved her, if she knew he'd do anything to keep her…

"Daisy, I…" he began.

Lily came storming through the door. "You won't believe it! Miss Vivian and that psycho are chatting it up like lifelong buds, and she's not ready to go. The psycho said she'd have someone drive her guest home later."

"Miss Vivian was okay with that?" Daisy asked, more than a little confused.

"More than okay. She's fine here, trust me." The middle Bell sister stormed past Jacob without acknowledging his existence. "Let's get the hell out of here."

Daisy nodded, and Jacob watched as she got in the car. The passenger seat. Lily jumped behind the wheel and took the keys from her big sister. Just as well, Jacob supposed. Daisy was badly shaken and had no business driving. He could see the women through the windshield, watched as the engine revved and the car slowly backed away and made a sharp one-eighty. Daisy never so much as lifted her head to look his way.

Jacob stood there and watched the taillights fade away. His frustration grew, second by second. He wanted to do something; he needed to fix this mess…but it wasn't an easy fix. He couldn't buy a solution or hire a team to make things right.

They were back to square one, just like that. He was leaving town without Daisy. And this time, she was leaving without him.

Everyone who came into the shop on Saturday wanted to know about Daisy's move to Atlanta. Daisy smiled a lot. She never hinted that the relocation was anything other than something she desperately wanted to do. She didn't complain about the space being sold out from under her, or an old woman's lies to get her way, or Jacob breaking her heart all over again. Instead she talked about being closer to concerts and ball games and shopping. She told everyone she'd probably lease a chair at a salon in Atlanta. More than a few customers said they'd still come to her to get their hair done, even though they'd have to pass a lot of salons along the way to get to her.

She was flattered, and pleased, and more than a little teary-eyed. Maybe her subconscious motives for staying put had been wrong-minded, but she had a lot of friends here, friends who had become like family over the years.

It was Lily who called a local real estate agent and made an appointment for that afternoon, after the shop closed. Houses didn't exactly fly off the market in Bell Grove, but by signing the papers she'd set things into motion.

Daisy only thought about Jacob every ten minutes or so, which was an improvement over the mostly sleepless night before, when she'd almost felt as if he were still lying beside her.

Her anger had faded as she'd tossed and turned, and by morning she'd been left more sad than anything else. Still embarrassed to be such a fool, hurt that she'd been used as a patsy, but mostly she was just sad.

As she walked through the house the real estate agent— a middle-aged man who was fond of telling bad jokes—

suggested improvements that would make the house more attractive to potential buyers. New wall colors, decluttering, new appliances. He told her how much more she'd get for the house if she made those improvements.

He made a suggestion about paint color as they stood in the doorway of her bedroom. Daisy couldn't see a new color on the walls. Instead she saw Jacob in her bed. She saw the two of them dancing in the dark, her skin against his, the music washing over them. She saw herself, thinking—*knowing*—that she still loved Jacob and couldn't live without him. It would take weeks, maybe months, to make all the changes the agent suggested. She didn't want to drag this painful process out any longer than was absolutely necessary.

She'd kept the house almost exactly as it had been when her parents had died. Someone else would have to remake it into something new and different.

"Put the house on the market as is," she said as she and the real estate agent sat at the kitchen table with a stack of papers between them.

"But you could get…"

"I don't care," she interrupted sharply, not caring—too much—that she sounded almost rude. She just wanted out, as soon as possible. She didn't want to spend weekend after weekend here painting and remodeling. No, she wanted to escape every memory—the good and the bad. Now. "Get what you can for it, that's all I ask."

He shook his head and pushed some papers toward her. She signed, blinking twice to clear the annoying tears from her eyes.

Jacob was accustomed to sleeping in hotel rooms, but the one he woke in late Saturday morning was not exactly up to his usual standards. The bed was hard, there was the unmistakable hum of the interstate too close by and the walls were so thin he could hear the television—and some of the conversation—in the room next door. The hotel he had chosen was close, right off the interstate in between Bell Grove and Atlanta. He was tempted to get in his car and head a little farther south so he could get on a plane and return to San Francisco today.

Instead of hopping out of bed and doing just that he lay there for a while. Running away was too easy; it was the coward's way out. It would be so easy to fly away from this mess and tell himself that he and Daisy just weren't meant to be. Soon enough he'd be back in the swing of things, and he'd relegate her to the back of his mind, as best he could. He'd bury himself in work, and tell himself it was all for the best. But Daisy was worth fighting for. He knew that, now. He wasn't at all sure that she wanted to be won—not by him, at least—but if he didn't try he'd always wonder.

He wasn't going to San Francisco without her, not without a fight. The life he'd lived for the past seven years, the job, the money, the travel, the excitement…it didn't look very attractive to him anymore. In fact, from a distance it looked downright sad.

It would be very easy to hop on a plane and resume his life as it had been before. Daisy would be fine. She had her sisters, and a million friends who would be there for her if she needed them. No matter what had happened in the past couple of weeks—the good and the bad—they could both return to the lives they'd made in the past seven years. And they'd grow apart all over again. It would hurt more, this time, but life would go on.

Jacob showered, he dressed, he walked to the restaurant next to the hotel for a big breakfast. Back in the hotel room he sat at the faux-wood desk with a crappy cup of

in-room coffee and answered a few of the emails that had
piled up during his vacation. There were enough messages
in his in-box to keep him busy for a week.

When Ted called that afternoon, Jacob wasn't at all surprised to hear that it had been his grandmother who'd set
the sale of a strip of downtown Bell Grove into motion.
And all this time he'd been feeling sorry for her...

"Thanks," Jacob said. He wheeled the creaky desk chair
around and ran anxious fingers through his hair, trying to
decide what to do. Usually he knew exactly what should
come next. That was his job, after all. In business, though,
not in life. His life held no surprises, no tough personal
choices.

Before he hung up the phone he said, "There's something else..."

Eunice sat in her favorite spot, staring out the window.
It was a beautiful summer day, bright and green. She half
hoped to see Jacob's rental car heading down the long,
winding driveway, but no such luck.

He hated her. She couldn't blame him. Well, she could
blame him a little. Why couldn't he—and everyone else—
see that her intentions had been good? She wondered if
he'd ever give her the opportunity to explain herself. If
he'd ever forgive her.

It was after lunch when she saw a bit of dust kicked up
in the distance. With her eyes squinted so she could see
farther, she waited to see who was coming this way. She
hoped for Jacob. She even said a quick prayer that her
grandson was coming home to make things right. Instead
her tired old eyes eventually identified an ancient pickup
truck she had never seen before. It was one Jacob wouldn't
be caught dead in, she knew that much. The vehicle she
watched left the driveway often, jerking off the asphalt

and then back on again, sending dirt and dust flying each time the wheels left the path.

A drunkard, Eunice thought. A lost drunkard who could not keep control of his vehicle. It was a rusted pickup, she noted as it jerked to a stop at the front of the house. Perhaps it had once been red; it was difficult to tell.

The very loud engine was silenced with a sputter. The driver's door opened with a rusty squeal, and—surprise—Vivian stepped out of the truck.

Eunice was at once envious of her old friend for being so limber—and able to drive at all—and at the same time she was furious that someone who drove so badly would get on the road. She could've been killed!

A small brown dog followed Vivian out of the vehicle. Eunice was horrified. She would not allow that filthy creature into the house!

She heard the doorbell, moved her chair away from the window and pretended to be surprised when Lurlene knocked on her door and introduced the guest.

The dog followed Vivian into the room, ran toward Eunice and—horrors—jumped into her lap.

"Oh, oh, oh." Eunice attempted to move her face away from the mutt's slobbering attempts to lick her on the mouth. She failed miserably.

"Settle down," Vivian said with a smile. "Buster is an affectionate animal. And besides, you should be glad that *someone* still likes you."

"Take him! Take him! Get this creature off me!"

Vivian chuckled as she reached out and grabbed the dog, who gratefully turned his attentions to her. She smiled as Buster licked her face and then settled into her arms, a dirty bundle of long brown hair. The animal apparently didn't have a care in the world.

"What kind of dog is that?" Eunice asked with disdain.

"Buster is a mutt."

"I see."

"Don't turn up your nose that way. There's nothing wrong with being a mutt. You need to get that stick out of your ass, Eunice." Vivian sat on the edge of the bed and placed the dog beside her.

Eunice bit back a command to get the *mutt* off her bedspread. But the damage was already done, and since the animal settled down in one place and didn't seem inclined to romp further, she let the infraction go.

"Did you apologize to Jacob?" Vivian asked.

Eunice felt her lips tighten and thin. "No. He left last night without seeing me, and he's not answering his cell phone." Not to her, at least. He had caller ID—everyone did these days—and he might be purposely avoiding her. Might be? Of course he was purposely avoiding her.

"Did you call Daisy?"

It took everything Eunice had not to drop her head in shame. "No. I...what can I say to her? How can I explain over the phone what I did and why? I really did have her best interests at heart, but she won't believe that." Besides, Daisy was almost certain to screen her calls just as Jacob did. If she tried calling from another phone, well, Daisy would surely just hang up when she answered and heard Eunice's voice on the line.

"You can start with *I'm sorry.*"

Those words did not come easily to Eunice. They never had.

"You need to stick with the truth," Vivian instructed dryly. "Think of telling the truth as a new experience. Prove to your family that you're an old dog who can learn new tricks."

Eunice was tempted to kick Vivian and her mangy dog out of the house. No one spoke to her this way! But she couldn't deny that she perversely liked having the plain-spoken Vivian back in her life. Last night they'd talked for hours, catching up on the time that had passed. It made Eunice regret deeply the lost years, the years they could've been friends if she'd only made the first move and said she was sorry.

"That's not going to be easy."

Vivian snorted. Such unladylike behavior! "Try actually having dementia, if you want to imagine something that's not easy. Remember Jean from our class? She died five years ago, but not until she'd forgotten everyone in her family, not until she'd completely lost touch with the world she lived in. You *pretended* because it suited your purpose. She lived with it. For years. Her family truly suffered, the way you made your family suffer because you wanted to get your way."

A sharp retort was on Eunice's tongue, but she bit it back. Jean? She hadn't seen or heard about Jean for years, but she still remembered her as a pretty young woman with a husband who loved her and a handful of rowdy kids. The family had moved to Chattanooga years ago, but maybe she'd moved back. Maybe Vivian had kept in touch all these years. Eunice fought back tears. Had she lost touch so completely with the world around her?

"I didn't mean to make light of…I just didn't think… was it bad for her, really?" Pretending not to remember had been convenient and—yes, she'd admit it—occasionally fun. But even to imagine truly being in that state was painful.

"It was bad." Vivian stroked her mutt's fur and looked away for a few moments. The silence that followed was maddening.

"You'll stay for dinner," Eunice said as she regained complete control of her emotions.

Vivian's head snapped around and her eyebrows shot up sharply. "I will?"

Eunice took a deep breath. Good heavens, this was difficult. "Vivian, would you *please* stay for dinner?"

"I don't know. I don't like to drive after dark."

"From what I saw, you shouldn't drive by the light of day, either," Eunice snapped.

Vivian glanced toward the window that looked out over the front of the house. "You saw me coming and then pretended to be surprised. Why?"

"I don't know," Eunice admitted. Had lying become the norm for her? Was it her natural mode of operation? "I suppose I don't want everyone to know that I sit here at the window and watch life pass me by."

Vivian nodded as if she understood. "I don't drive often, and I will admit, that old thing doesn't steer the way it used to."

"I'll ask Caleb to look at it," Eunice said. "He's always been quite good with cars. He and Jacob both, though of course Jacob isn't here." She cleared her throat. "Caleb can drive you home later tonight." She added, in a lowered voice, "If that's all right with you, of course."

"Fine by me." Vivian looked pointedly at the wheelchair. "Since I'll be here for a while, I have some exercises I want you to try."

"Exercises?" Eunice repeated sharply. "I'll have you know, I do *not* exercise."

Vivian harrumphed, and there went those eyebrows again. "Maybe that's why you're in a wheelchair."

Dogs, exercise, apologizing. Eunice very much wanted her old friend back in her life, but she had a feeling that if she gave in nothing would ever be the same. Exercise! Horrors.

"The Braves are playing a day game today," Vivian said,

heading for the small television Eunice rarely bothered to turn on. "You do have cable, don't you?"

Baseball? Oh, the sacrifices…

"Of course," Eunice said.

"We'll exercise between innings, and after the game we'll try making those phone calls."

As much as Eunice hated the thought of talking to Jacob or Daisy, of facing what she'd done, she knew her old friend, who was perhaps going to become a new friend, was right.

Chapter Sixteen

Daisy wanted to be happy about leaving Bell Grove; she wanted to be excited about all the changes that were coming to her life. Goodness knows she needed a few changes!

But after Lily left—she didn't have any more time off from her new job—Daisy found herself sinking deeper and deeper into a funk. She waffled back and forth between trying to psych herself up, and being in the dumps about leaving home. Mari and Lily didn't complain about getting homesick. They didn't pine for Bell Grove. They hadn't put their lives on hold to keep what was left of their parents alive. She had. What was wrong with her?

Then again, they both knew this house and their big sister would be here, waiting for them, if they ever did get the urge to come home.

No more. As she packed knickknacks and doodads that hadn't been moved in many years, Daisy found herself getting maudlin. Every piece she touched had a memory attached to it. They'd gone in together and given their mother this figurine for Mother's Day one year. It was cheap and, yes, a little tacky, but Mom had loved it. At the very least, she'd pretended well to love it. It had been sitting on the same shelf for seventeen years.

This vase was chipped, thanks to a rambunctious four-year-old Lily. It was always placed with the chipped side to the wall, so no one would see the defect. This cat figurine had belonged to their grandmother—their father's mother. Mari had always loved it. Every dish, every plate, every cloth napkin had a memory attached to it.

Packing things away was torture. Daisy wasn't ready to sell or toss the worthless treasures, but where was she going to store it all?

She tried to make piles. Definitely keep, maybe throw away, Mari or Lily might want. But she kept moving things out of the *maybe throw away* pile and into one of the others. At one point she conceded that she was a hopeless pack rat and her sisters were going to have to help her make decisions about all this *stuff.*

She sat cross-legged on the living room floor, a trio of small framed pictures lined up before her. Mari, Lily and Daisy, each of them at one year old. These she'd take with her, she decided. No matter where she lived, she could look at these photos every day. They were a part of home she could take with her.

There wouldn't be room for everything, though, and she didn't want her new home to look exactly like the old one. It wouldn't look new at all, if that was the case. And oh, she really needed *new.* A fresh start, a new life. She'd decided that was such a good idea, and now it terrified her. Just a little.

Daisy lifted her head when she heard a car pull into her driveway. The engine was unfamiliar. Funny how it didn't take long to identify the particular sound of a car. It wasn't Lily's car, not Mari's truck, not Jacob's rental— thank goodness. Who else could it be? If the real estate agent wanted to show the house, he really should've called first. A pile of knickknacks on the living room floor wasn't exactly proper staging.

She stood and went to the window, brushing her dusty hands on her shorts as she went, and pulled back the curtain to peek outside. The car parked behind hers was a large black sedan, a few years old but in pristine condition. The black paint shone, the chrome grill sparkled, as if no bug would dare to die there.

Caleb Tasker stepped out of the driver's side of the tank of a car that was parked in the driveway, and Daisy's heart did a sick flip. Had Jacob sent him? No, that would be so unlike Jacob, to send someone else to do his dirty work for him. Well, unless this was a new MO for him. Maybe the business hotshot ordered people to do his dirty work all the time. She couldn't imagine Caleb stopping by to chat with her; they didn't know one another well at all. All they had in common was Jacob.

The rear passenger door opened, and Miss Vivian stepped out. She wore a Sunday dress and her hair was braided. Not as neatly as if Daisy had done the job, but she had made an effort.

Daisy was surprised. She never would've guessed either of the two of them would come to see her at the house, and together? No way. Had Miss Vivian called Caleb and asked him to give her a ride to town? Did she think Daisy would leave without saying goodbye?

The big surprise came when Caleb opened the front passenger door and assisted an unsteady Eunice Tasker from the vehicle.

Daisy let the curtain drop. Of all the people she didn't

want to see right now, Miss Eunice was second only to Jacob. Maybe if she'd taken one of the phone calls from the Tasker House earlier in the day, she wouldn't have Miss Eunice knocking on her door.

It took several minutes for the doorbell to ring. Daisy stood in the center of the room, away from the window and the door. She seriously considered not answering the door, the way she hadn't answered the phone. She didn't want to be a coward, even if she felt very cowardly at the moment.

She finally took a deep breath and walked to the door, just as the doorbell sounded again. Just because they were on her front porch, that didn't mean she had to invite them in. This was still her house. She'd find out what they wanted, then coolly and calmly send them all on their way.

"Thank goodness," Miss Eunice said breathlessly as the door swung open. "I desperately need to sit."

Caleb supported her on one side, Miss Vivian on the other. The unsteady woman really did look as if she were about to fall.

Daisy held the door open and allowed the three to walk inside. So much for her grand plan of sending them away! The two on either side of Miss Eunice led her to the nearest chair, where she sat carefully and with evident relief. She closed her eyes, took a deep breath and sank down into the chair. Finally she opened her eyes and looked directly at Daisy.

"Vivian has insisted that I *walk*," Eunice said with disdain.

"She's got no strength in her legs at all," Vivian said.

"It's hard!" Eunice argued.

"Well, it'll only get harder if you don't move."

"She made me exercise and watch *baseball*," Eunice grumbled, pursing her lips in evident displeasure.

Vivian responded. "The exercise is good for you, and trust me, baseball will grow on you."

The two women bickered like sisters. It was very odd. And why did they have to bicker *here*?

"May I help you?" Daisy asked formally. That seemed better than what she really wanted to say. *What the hell do you want*?

Eunice looked up at her grandson. "Caleb, go wait in the car."

Caleb couldn't get out of the house fast enough. He did cast Daisy an apologetic glance, but there was too much humor in his eyes for her to believe he was truly sympathetic. When he was gone, Miss Eunice looked at Daisy again. Her eyes were hard, inflexible, which made her words all the more surprising.

"I'm sorry." The simple words were clipped and emotionless.

Daisy didn't know what to say to that, so she said nothing.

"For..." Vivian nudged gently.

"For interfering, for lying, for basically sticking my nose in where it didn't belong." Eunice's words were sharp. Apologizing was obviously a new experience for her. She wasn't very good at it, and she had to follow up with a qualifier. "But that doesn't mean I wasn't right. You and Jacob do have feelings for one another, and if I hadn't done what I did you'd never know."

I don't want to know.

"Tell her the rest," Vivian urged.

"If you'll stay, I'll let you remain in your space downtown rent free."

"Eunice!" Vivian snapped.

The woman in the chair waved a dismissive hand. "Fine, I'll give it to you, free and clear. I'll put that entire side of downtown Bell Grove in your name and you can do with it what you please. If you stay, of course. I considered just calling off the deal to buy the property, but I understand that's not what you want."

Daisy shook her head. "I'm leaving town, and nothing you say or do will change my mind." And the truth was, she didn't want anything from the Taskers. She tried to sound tough and uncaring as she added, "I don't care what you do with that building." What she didn't say was *Choke on it*.

She looked at Vivian, who was obviously a part of this ridiculous scheme because she wanted Daisy to stay. "Don't worry, Miss Vivian. There are lots of other volunteers, and I'll make arrangements for someone else to get your groceries and take you to the doctor."

"I can drive myself."

Daisy shook her head. "Miss Vivian, I've seen you drive. Please let me make other arrangements."

"That won't be necessary," Eunice said sharply. "Vivian will soon be moving into Tasker House."

"I don't think so," Vivian grumbled.

Eunice didn't back down. "Lurlene is getting on in years and she needs some help. With Vivian as my live-in companion, Lurlene will have more free time. And I'll have someone around who makes me do things others won't."

"Like exercising," Vivian said.

"And apologizing," Eunice added. "There's always someone around to drive, so we can save the county from Vivian's dreadful attempts behind the wheel. Besides, we get the Braves games in that High Definition television. Vivian likes that. She likes looking at the players' butts in those tight pants."

"Eunice!" Vivian actually blushed a bit.

"Well, it's true enough. Besides, I don't like the idea of her living out there in the middle of nowhere all alone."

"I'm not alone. I have Buster."

Daisy didn't feel the need to walk on eggs, not with these two. "I thought y'all hated each other!"

"We got over it," Vivian said. "Life is too short to spend it wallowing in regret. Mistakes were made on both sides, but we've decided to move on. It's not like either one of us has so many friends left that we can throw one over in the name of spite."

Eunice gave Daisy her full attention once again. "So, will you consider staying?"

Daisy shook her head.

"Think it over," Miss Vivian said. "You'll be missed if you leave. Bell Grove won't be the same without you. You're the last of the Bells here and that means something."

Eunice looked squarely at Daisy, her old eyes still strong and smart. "Tell me you don't love Jacob. If you can do that, I'll walk away and never bother you again."

Daisy opened her mouth, fully intending to say the words, to tell Miss Eunice, and herself, that she didn't love Jacob. Didn't need him, didn't want him. But she choked on the unspoken words. They lodged in her throat, left her helpless and scared. She did love him, but what good had that done her?

The old woman nodded once, satisfied.

Vivian went to the front door, opened it and called to Caleb. Together they assisted Eunice from the chair and held on to her as they moved across the porch and down the stairs—carefully and slowly—and finally into the car. Daisy stood on the porch for a long time after the car had driven away.

She left her piles of stuff sitting on the living room floor, unsorted and unpacked, and sat in the front porch rocker. When she moved to Atlanta, there would be no quiet moments like this one. Atlanta was always hopping; there were so many *people* there. At the same time, she knew moving on was the right decision.

She also admitted, reluctantly, that she was still in love with Jacob and probably always would be. Tasker or not, lousy white knight, horrible guitar player who had the bad judgment to wear suits in Bell Grove in the summertime... she loved him. That was the reason she suffered doubts about moving away, that was why starting over in Atlanta practically gave her hives.

In her heart she had never imagined she'd leave Bell Grove and start over without him.

Jacob returned to Tasker House, moving back into his room and avoiding family members as he did what needed to be done. In between phone calls and long emails, he attempted to play the guitar that had been sitting in his closet for seven years. He'd lost his touch, and he had no calluses on his fingers, but there was something there, still. If he made the effort, if he practiced regularly, he'd soon be playing again. He'd never play in public, but that had never been his ambition anyway. He just wanted to make music, now and then.

He hadn't taken the guitar with him to San Francisco, but it wasn't like he couldn't have bought another guitar there. He hadn't done that. He'd given up the pastime, years ago, maybe because he had never been all that good at playing, maybe because he would never be more than adequate when it came to music.

How many nights had he played for Daisy while she'd sung along? After class, before bed, in the middle of the night...in their rare spare time, while they'd pursued an education. She sang as badly as he played, just slightly out of tune and with the occasional missed lyric or note. And yet, those had been good times. Maybe the best.

When his fingers gave out, Jacob returned the guitar to the case that had been sitting in his closet for the past seven years. He opened the small compartment built into the case for picks, and found something else he'd stored there. Something else he'd packed away and all but forgotten.

He had a lot to relearn, after spending seven years chasing a career that had been financially rewarding while it suffocated everything else in his life. More than playing the guitar and getting grease under his fingernails and learning to deal with his dysfunctional family more than once every five years. He'd gotten so sucked into the corporate lifestyle he'd forgotten that there was more to be had from life. Much more. He'd set the most important aspects of life to the side.

It was almost dark when he made the final arrangements and left the house, headed into Bell Grove to make the most important deal of his lifetime.

Daisy sat on the couch, numb and lost. She didn't turn on the television, didn't pack her suitcase...didn't fix herself supper, trying to use up the rest of the fresh food in the kitchen. There were still three piles of stuff on the floor. The pile of things to throw away was dismally small, but time was running out and she had to get busy.

Yeah, time was really running out. The house had sold. She'd hoped it would, of course, but houses didn't move that quickly in Bell Grove and she'd expected to have more time. Time to get ready, maybe even time to change her mind. She couldn't even turn the offer down, because it was for more than she'd asked. The buyer hadn't even bothered to look at the inside of the house! The real estate agent was thrilled. Two offers on his listings in one day had put him over the moon.

She wondered who else had sold their home, who else, besides her, was leaving Bell Grove.

She was so tempted to get in her car and drive out to Tasker House, see if Jacob was still there. If she found him there, would she be brave enough to tell him what she really felt? Was she brave enough to go after what she wanted?

Maybe *she* could be the white knight.

No, he'd said he wasn't going to stay. He was probably back in California, already putting the disastrous events of his trip home behind him.

Everything hadn't been disastrous…

When the car pulled into her driveway, her heart skipped a beat. Her ear for engines—thanks to her dad— told her that was Jacob's rental car. As she had earlier in the day when Miss Eunice had come calling, she sat there and considered not answering the doorbell when it rang. What could he possibly want? Had he left something behind? A razor, a toothbrush…*her?*

She waited, and waited, but the doorbell didn't ring.

After several minutes she heard the muted strum of a guitar, the sound faded since the windows and doors were closed, but unmistakable. One slightly out of tune guitar playing a tune that reminded her vaguely of mariachi music. And playing badly.

She sat there a moment, her emotions in a jumble, then jumped off the couch and ran for the front door and the porch just beyond.

Jacob sat on the steps, dressed in jeans and a T-shirt, his back to her as he gave his full attention to the less-than-perfect notes. He didn't turn to look at her, though he must've heard her. She hadn't tried to be quiet, didn't try to sneak up on him.

Looking at his back, and the slightly mussed dark hair and the cut of his shoulders, a certainty washed over her. Certainty and relief and a sense of being whole for the first time in a very long time. He'd broken her heart and made her love him all over again. His family was big and interfering and, simply put, a pain in the ass. He might break her heart all over again, if she gave him the chance.

But she couldn't imagine moving forward without Jacob in her life in some way. As a friend, as more than a friend. She needed him.

The mariachi attempt ended, thank goodness, and he started something new. She remembered this song, recognized it even though he pretty much butchered every note. It was the song they'd danced to just last week.

"You were never very good, but I have to say, you've gotten worse," she said as she approached him.

"I know. I need more practice." He glanced over his shoulder, and his dark gaze cut through her. "I need to practice quite a few things I've lost touch with."

Daisy sat beside Jacob, not too close, but close enough. She'd been running away, not just from Miss Eunice's lies, not just from a life that had gotten stale, but from Jacob and everything he represented. She'd never stopped loving him, and in spite of everything that had happened here he was literally on her doorstep.

Her gallon of death-by-chocolate ice cream. Her first love. Her past. Maybe her future?

She blamed him and his family for the fiasco, but she had to face the truth that she shared some of the blame. When she'd heard the name *Tasker,* she'd been so certain Jacob was the one behind the sale of that downtown

property. She'd condemned him without asking for an explanation.

She'd torn them apart before he could break her heart
again.

All day she'd been thinking about her life, her mistakes…the rut she was in of her own free will. After Miss
Eunice's visit, she'd been forced to think about other
things, as well. Most of all she'd thought about Jacob. She
loved him and she always had. She was in a rut because
he was no longer hers. Since Lily and Mari had left home,
she hadn't just been keeping their old life alive, she'd been
sitting here *waiting* for Jacob to come for her. She hadn't
realized it, and if she had she would've been horrified, but
it all made sense to her now.

"Ask me again to go to San Francisco with you," she
whispered. This time she'd say yes, she'd throw away everything to be with Jacob.

"I can't," he said. He stopped playing and put the guitar aside.

Daisy's heart broke all over again. He hadn't forgiven
her for not trusting him, for thinking the worst. Why
should she expect anything different? Thank goodness
he didn't allow her to suffer for very long.

"I'm not going back to San Francisco. Not for very long,
anyway. There will be things to take care of, I suppose."

"What are you talking about?"

"I quit my job," he said. Jacob looked at her, really
looked at her for the first time since she'd walked out of
the house, and her heart flipped wildly in her chest. She
loved him, she liked him; she could even forgive him for
being a Tasker…

"You did *what?*"

"Well, I tried to quit. I've been on the phone all day,
and as it stands now I'm going to work freelance for the

company. I'm now a consultant. That means I can live wherever the hell I want to. My boss is very unhappy, but he'll learn to live with the change. We'll make it work."

He sounded so calm, so reasonable, and the truth became clear to her. "You're the one who bought my house!"

Jacob nodded. "I did. I also bought the old Hamilton place. We need a home of our own, Daisy, a home that's *ours,* but I thought you might want to hang on to this house, too. Your sisters might want to stay here, now and then."

The old Hamilton place was a grand two-story colonial on the edge of town. She'd always loved that house, and Jacob knew it. No one knew her the way he did.

"A home of our own?" she repeated.

"I also bought a condo in Buckhead. The Hamilton house needs a lot of work, and I wasn't sure where you'd prefer to live, here or in Atlanta. If you want to live somewhere else just tell me. We can live anywhere, and when I do have to travel you can come with me, if it suits you. Or you can stay here and we'll talk on the phone for hours while I'm gone, or you can visit your sisters, or stay at the condo. Whatever you want, whatever you need. You're my number-one priority, Daisy, you will always come first. I won't forget that again."

Her mind continued to spin. "You bought a house and a condo? For *us?*"

"If you'll have me." Jacob reached into the open guitar case, opened a small compartment that was built into one side and drew out a small velvet box. He got on one knee so they were face-to-face. Daisy's heart thumped. This was happening too fast! She wasn't ready! It was too soon!

She took a deep breath and her heart resumed a fairly normal rhythm. No, it wasn't too soon, not at all. In fact, this was overdue. They'd both waited more than long enough.

Jacob opened the box and offered it to her on his open palm. A simple diamond solitaire set in yellow gold winked at her. The stone was a good size, but was far from ostentatious. "Daisy Bell, I love you. I have always loved you. Will you marry me?"

Her heart caught in her throat; her mouth went dry. Finally she choked out a soft, "Yes."

Jacob smiled, as he crept up the steps to take her hand and place the ring on her finger. "I hope you like it."

"I do, very much. It's perfect." She kissed him, once. Again.

Jacob drew away slightly and looked into her eyes. "Good. It's been sitting in this guitar case for seven years." He leaned in and kissed her again, his lips soft and warm against hers.

She enjoyed the kiss for a moment then she pulled away. "Seven years? Jacob!"

He shrugged his shoulders, and with one finger moved a strand of hair off her shoulder. "Seven years. I saw the ring and knew it was right for you, so I bought it. I kept trying to plan the perfect proposal, but nothing ever seemed quite right. Besides, I wasn't in a rush. I thought we had all the time in the world. We were so young, and all I could see ahead of us was blue skies."

"And then my parents died," Daisy whispered.

Jacob nodded. "Everything fell apart after that. I couldn't give you an engagement ring right after your folks died, and I didn't want to propose and then move to the other side of the country. My plans to come home at Christmas didn't work out, but for a long time I still believed that we had all the time in the world, that nothing would change for us. I waited for the perfect moment, and it never came. You know the rest. I'm sorry it took me so long to put that ring on your finger, where it belongs. I love you, Daisy. I need you. I don't care where we live, as long as I get to live with you."

She draped her arms around his neck. "I love you, too."

Her last name was going to be Tasker. Maybe that wouldn't be so bad, after all.

She kissed Jacob again, wallowed in the kiss, and when she pulled away she placed her forehead against his and smiled.

They'd waited long enough, and this moment was as perfect as it could possibly get.

"I hope you don't have a long engagement in mind…"

Chapter Seventeen

"I told you so," Eunice whispered to Vivian, as they sat near the foot of the stairs, waiting. She was seated in a comfortable wing chair, as was her friend. The wheelchair was parked in her bedroom, and while she might need it by the end of the day, she didn't need it right now. Eunice had been surprised by how much she could do when her friend pushed her.

"Don't brag, Eunice," Vivian responded, her voice low. "It's not attractive."

Vivian had moved into Tasker House a few days earlier, at Eunice's insistence. She'd brought her little dog, Buster, with her. The mutt was not as annoying as Eunice had initially thought it would be. In fact, Buster was a very loving and loyal animal, and he was surprisingly smart. She allowed the dog to sit on the foot of the bed when they ate chocolate-covered cherries, or watched a baseball game. She and Vivian were already planning a trip to Atlanta to watch a game in person, as soon as Eunice was able to get around a bit better. With Vivian's help, she grew stronger every day. Caleb, who loved baseball, had promised to take them.

Eunice had to admit—silently and only to herself—that she wasn't always right. Maddy hadn't forgiven her the way Daisy had, but she was here for the reunion. Eunice had watched and listened a lot during the reunion. Others in the family seemed to genuinely like Maddy. Maybe she didn't dress properly, and maybe she did wear too much makeup, and goodness knows she'd never be a brain surgeon, but she was friendly and sunny. She and Ben had shared big news this weekend; they were going to have a baby. The Tasker family was growing once again. Eunice hadn't given up on earning the girl's forgiveness. One day.

Finally the music began. Not a recording, but a live string quartet. Eunice could get things done right *and* in a hurry, if need be.

Lily and Mari walked down the stairs slowly. Daisy's sisters both wore yellow sundresses, though they were not identical. Jacob elbowed his brother in the ribs when Caleb whistled and muttered an appreciative, drawled, "Damn." Those who were close enough to hear laughed lightly.

Eunice was not amused. Neither of the available Bell girls would be appropriate for Caleb! Mari was too young, and Lily was too harsh and outspoken. No, she'd need to look elsewhere for a bride for Caleb. And soon.

When Lily and Mari reached the foot of the stairs, Daisy appeared at the top. Eunice smiled. Her wedding gown fit Daisy perfectly. No adjustments had been required. That was a good thing, given the short time they'd had to pull this wedding ceremony together. The bride's hair was down, simple and unadorned, and she carried white and yellow roses.

Daisy walked down the stairs slowly. Even though the foyer and the hallways beyond were filled with people, her smile and eyes were for Jacob alone. When she reached her waiting groom she whispered, before the preacher said a single word, "I do, I do, I do."

And Eunice turned once more to her friend, a smug smile on her face. "I told you so."

* * * * *

COMING NEXT MONTH from Harlequin®
Special Edition®
AVAILABLE AUGUST 21, 2012

#2209 THE PRODIGAL COWBOY
Kathleen Eagle

Working with Ethan is more challenging than investigative reporter Bella ever dreamed. He's as irresistible as ever, and he has his own buried secrets.

#2210 REAL VINTAGE MAVERICK
Montana Mavericks: Back in the Saddle
Marie Ferrarella

A widowed rancher has given up on love—until he meets a shop owner who believes in second chances. Can she get the cowboy to see it for himself?

#2211 THE DOCTOR'S DO-OVER
Summer Sisters
Karen Templeton

As a kid, he would have done anything to make her happy, to keep her safe. As an adult, is he enough of a man to let her do the same for him?

#2212 THE COWBOY'S FAMILY PLAN
Brighton Valley Babies
Judy Duarte

A doctor and aspiring mother agrees to help a cowboy looking for a surrogate—and falls in love with him.

#2213 THE DOCTOR'S CALLING
Men of the West
Stella Bagwell

Veterinary assistant Laurel Stanton must decide if she should follow her boss and hang on to a hopeless love for him...or move on to a new life.

#2214 TEXAS WEDDING
Celebrations, Inc.
Nancy Robards Thompson

When she opens her own catering company, AJ Sherwood-Antonelli's professional dreams are finally coming true. The last thing she needs is to fall for a hunky soldier who doesn't want to stay in one place long enough put down roots....

You can find more information on upcoming Harlequin® titles, free excerpts and more at www.HarlequinInsideRomance.com.

HSECNM0812

REQUEST YOUR FREE BOOKS!

2 FREE NOVELS PLUS 2 FREE GIFTS!

❦ Harlequin®

SPECIAL EDITION

Life, Love & Family

YES! Please send me 2 FREE Harlequin® Special Edition novels and my 2 FREE gifts (gifts are worth about $10). After receiving them, if I don't wish to receive any more books, I can return the shipping statement marked "cancel." If I don't cancel, I will receive 6 brand-new novels every month and be billed just $4.49 per book in the U.S. or $5.24 per book in Canada. That's a saving of at least 14% off the cover price! It's quite a bargain! Shipping and handling is just 50¢ per book in the U.S. and 75¢ per book in Canada.* I understand that accepting the 2 free books and gifts places me under no obligation to buy anything. I can always return a shipment and cancel at any time. Even if I never buy another book, the two free books and gifts are mine to keep forever.

235/335 HDN FEGF

Name _____ (PLEASE PRINT)

Address _____ Apt. #

City _____ State/Prov. _____ Zip/Postal Code

Signature (if under 18, a parent or guardian must sign)

Mail to the **Reader Service:**
IN U.S.A.: P.O. Box 1867, Buffalo, NY 14240-1867
IN CANADA: P.O. Box 609, Fort Erie, Ontario L2A 5X3

Not valid for current subscribers to Harlequin Special Edition books.

Want to try two free books from another line?
Call 1-800-873-8635 or visit www.ReaderService.com.

* Terms and prices subject to change without notice. Prices do not include applicable taxes. Sales tax applicable in N.Y. Canadian residents will be charged applicable taxes. Offer not valid in Quebec. This offer is limited to one order per household. All orders subject to credit approval. Credit or debit balances in a customer's account(s) may be offset by any other outstanding balance owed by or to the customer. Please allow 4 to 6 weeks for delivery. Offer available while quantities last.

Your Privacy—The Reader Service is committed to protecting your privacy. Our Privacy Policy is available online at www.ReaderService.com or upon request from the Reader Service.

We make a portion of our mailing list available to reputable third parties that offer products we believe may interest you. If you prefer that we not exchange your name with third parties, or if you wish to clarify or modify your communication preferences, please visit us at www.ReaderService.com/consumerchoice or write to us at Reader Service Preference Service, P.O. Box 9062, Buffalo, NY 14269. Include your complete name and address.

HSE11B

SPECIAL EDITION

Life, Love and Family

NEW YORK TIMES BESTSELLING AUTHOR

KATHLEEN EAGLE

brings readers a story of a cowboy's return home

Ethan Wolf Track is a true cowboy—rugged, wild and commitment-free. He's returned home to South Dakota to rebuild his life, and he'll start by competing in Mustang Sally's Wild Horse Training Competition.... But TV reporter Bella Primeaux is on the hunt for a different kind of prize, and she'll do whatever it takes to uncover the truth.

THE PRODIGAL COWBOY

Available September 2012 wherever books are sold!

www.Harlequin.com

HSE65691

*Enjoy an exclusive excerpt
from Harlequin® Special Edition®
THE DOCTOR'S DO-OVER by Karen Templeton*

"What I actually said was that this doesn't make sense."

She cocked her head, frowning. "This?"

His eyes once again met hers. And held on tight.

Oh. This. Got it.

Except…she didn't.

Then he reached over to palm her jaw, making her breath catch and her heart trip an instant before he kissed her. Kissed her good. And hard. But good. Oh, so good, his tongue teasing hers in a way that made everything snap into focus and melt at the same time— Then he backed away, hand still on jaw, eyes still boring into hers. Tortured, what-the-heck-am-I-doing eyes. "If things had gone like I planned, this would've been where I dropped you off, said something about, yeah, I had a nice time, too, I'll call you, and driven away with no intention whatsoever of calling you—"

"With or without the kiss?"

"That kiss? Without."

O-kaay. "Noted. Except…you wouldn't do that."

His brow knotted. "Do what?"

"Tell me you'll call if you're not gonna. Because that is not how you roll, Patrick Shaughnessy."

He let go to let his head drop back against the headrest, emitting a short, rough laugh. "You're going to be the death of me."

"Not intentionally," she said, and he laughed again. But it was such a sad laugh tears sprang to April's eyes.

"No, tonight did not go as planned," he said. "In any way, shape, form or fashion. But weirdly enough in some ways it went better." Another humorless laugh. "Or would have, if you'd been a normal woman."

"As in, whiny and pouty."

"As in, not somebody who'd still be sitting here after what happened. Who would've been out of this truck before I'd even put it in Park. But here you are…" In the dim light, she saw his eyes glisten a moment before he turned, slamming his hand against the steering wheel.

"I don't want this, April! Don't want…you inside my head, seeing how messy it is in there! Don't want…"

He stopped, breathing hard, and April could practically hear him think, *Don't want my heart broken again.*

***

Look for
THE DOCTOR'S DO-OVER
by Karen Templeton
this September 2012 from Harlequin® Special Edition®.

Copyright © 2012 by Harlequin Books S.A.

HSEEXP0912

HARLEQUIN®

SO YOU THINK YOU CAN WRITE

Harlequin and Mills & Boon are joining forces in a global search for new authors.

In September 2012 we're launching our biggest contest yet—with the prize of being published by the world's leader in romance fiction!

Look for more information on our website, **www.soyouthinkyoucanwrite.com**

So you think you can write? Show us!

SYTYCW0912

The scandal continues
in The Santina Crown miniseries
with *USA TODAY* bestselling author

Sarah Morgan

Second in line to the throne, Matteo Santina
knows a thing or two about keeping his cool under
pressure. But when pop star singer Izzy Jackson
shows up to her sister's wedding and makes
a scandalous scene that goes against all royal
protocol, Matteo whisks her offstage, into his limo
and straight to his luxury palazzo.... Rumor has it
that they have yet to emerge!

DEFYING THE PRINCE

Available August 21 wherever books are sold!

www.Harlequin.com

HPI3090